"You don't trust me."

Shock went through  words. Betrayal eve existing under some deal with the girls. N

He was right to face acknowledge. Having the two of them as parents, sharing parenting duties, might not be best for Ruby and Violet in the long run.

She wanted to let anger take over.

Or persuasion.

But knew she wouldn't like herself if she did either.

"No, I don't," she said. But then words continued coming to her. "Not as far as I'm concerned. And yet, in a way, I do, in that I know what not to rely on. I know how you really feel now."

"You have no idea how I feel." Sounded a bit like he was letting anger do his talking. She waited a moment, but when he didn't continue, she did.

"I do trust you where the girls are concerned," she told him. "More than I'd trust anyone else." He needed to know that. "Even knowing how you feel about my life choices...and knowing that I could lose out...I trust you to do what you think is best for Ruby and Violet."

"What if what I think is best turns out not to be?"

Dear Reader,

The thought of you picking up this book and having it ahead of you to read makes me smile big for you! It was such a different and compelling story to write, loaded with emotion and tons of satisfaction, too.

Secret babies are huge in romance, but I've never read one where the mother is the one from whom the secret is kept. Doesn't even make sense that it could happen. But it did. Mia wakes up one morning in her normal life, and by that afternoon, there she is, with twin four-year-old daughters she didn't know she had. The turmoil that follows got me out of the bed and to the computer, eager to get back to them, every morning. Twelve pages from the end of this book, I didn't know how it was going to end. But Mia and Jordon had me covered.

And for those of you who've read my books for a while, you'll notice an old friend—the town where Mia lives. She grew up in Shelter Valley! If you've never been there and you like the town, you have fifteen other Shelter Valley stories, completely stand-apart from this one, waiting to take you back! A couple of the experts from Sierra's Web pay a visit, too!

Happy reading!

Tara Taylor Quinn

Their Secret Twins

TARA TAYLOR QUINN

HARLEQUIN
SPECIAL
EDITION

Recycling programs
for this product may
not exist in your area.

ISBN-13: 978-1-335-72477-9

Their Secret Twins

Copyright © 2023 by TTQ Books LLC

Harlequin Enterprises ULC
22 Adelaide St. West, 41st Floor
Toronto, Ontario M5H 4E3, Canada
www.Harlequin.com

Printed in U.S.A.

A *USA TODAY* bestselling author of over 105 novels in twenty languages, **Tara Taylor Quinn** has sold more than seven million copies. Known for her intense emotional fiction, Ms. Quinn's novels have received critical acclaim in the UK and most recently from Harvard. She is the recipient of the Readers' Choice Award and has appeared often on local and national TV, including *CBS Sunday Morning*.

For TTQ offers, news and contests, visit www.tarataylorquinn.com!

Books by Tara Taylor Quinn

Harlequin Special Edition

Shelter Valley Stories

Their Secret Twins

Sierra's Web

His Lost and Found Family
Reluctant Roommates
Her Best Friend's Baby

Furever Yours

Love off the Leash

The Parent Portal

Having the Soldier's Baby
A Baby Affair
Her Motherhood Wish
A Mother's Secrets

Visit the Author Profile page
at Harlequin.com for more titles.

For Baby Boy Sorrell, who isn't here yet as I write this, but who will be before the book is out. Welcome to the world, little guy, and to a family who is going to love you forever!

Chapter One

Who scheduled interviews for Saturday morning?
Oh, right, he did. Had. He'd done it.

Pulling himself out of a deep slumber, Jordon Lawrence came to, remembering why his alarm had gone off before nine on a weekend morning. He needed to hire a couple of financial advisors.

He'd shown attention-getting gains at the close of the market the day before. Had been on the floor to see the final results when the bell rang, and then had attended three different evening functions with celebrating clients—and potential clients. All gatherings had sported a full bar but none had included dinner.

Out of bed, Jordon made it to the kitchen for coffee, standing there in a robe and nothing else. He was sipping the hot liquid like it was saving his life when his doorman buzzed him.

He had a certified letter—had to go down and sign for it or pick it up in person himself at the post office.

Not wanting to stand in line at the post office—or worry about getting there during business hours—he climbed into last night's pants, slid his arms into the shirt he'd taken off as he'd fallen into bed, slipped his sockless feet into his wing tips, and grabbed his coffee to sip on the elevator ride down the eleven floors and then back up again.

That one cup hadn't been nearly enough.

An entire pot of espresso wouldn't have done it.

Sitting on the edge of his couch, still in the wrinkled clothes, Jordon stared at the letter he'd had in his possession for a full twenty minutes. Continued to stare.

He read it again, and then, his eyes glazing over, he blinked and read once more.

He didn't need to see the words to know verbatim what they said. He just had to wait another five minutes until it was officially 5:00 a.m. on the West Coast. In his mind, five designated morning hours during Arizona summer months. It was light by then. He'd call the number at the bottom of the letter at that time.

No way was he the father of four-year-old twins. Other than with Mia Jones, an eternity ago, he'd never even been in a long-term relationship.

Savannah Compton, JD, had the wrong guy.

And those poor little girls needed their deceased parents' lawyer to find the right one.

* * *

Finishing up the final touches on her latest boho wall hanging video, Mia Jones glanced at the phone resting on the big crafting table beside her as it rang. With an unusual loss of focus, she shook her head, pushed to decline the call and went back to work on the laptop she was using to edit her work. Surrounded by fancy camera paraphernalia, ring lights and soundproof headphones, she was a far cry from the woman Jordon Lawrence had known.

The family ranch he'd last seen failing stood tall and proud around her—with her as the sole owner. Her social media accounts had millions of followers and she still had a pile of invitations from crafting manufacturers to represent their products on her channels even after accepting more than thirty such offers.

The second time the phone rang, she jumped, accidentally deleting a couple of the clips she'd been adjusting. A glance told her that the caller was Jordon again.

She waited an extra ring before refusing that call, too.

She hadn't heard from the man in ten years, and he thought he could just beep into her life again in the middle of a beautiful summer Sunday afternoon? Didn't matter to her how much money he made or how important he was in New York. In Shelter Valley, on her property, he was just the guy who broke her heart.

She almost answered the third call. What if the guy was sick or something? Had he played the market a little too hard and lost everything that mattered to him?

And he thought he'd come crawling back to her, begging for the things he'd found less valuable when he'd left her to go to the big city and make his fortune?

He could be in serious trouble. What if he'd been hurt and needed help from the ranch's horse therapy program?

On the fourth ring, she declined that call, too.

There were plenty of ranches, plenty of therapy programs, plenty of people in the world who could help Jordon Lawrence.

She wasn't one of them.

And if he was calling for any other reason—for old times' sake, just to catch up, maybe he was going to be in Phoenix visiting his mother and was at a loose end—no thank you. With sugar on top.

On edge, waiting to see if there was a fifth call, Mia managed to recover her lost clips, finish the video and move it, along with the others she'd made that day, to her publishing queue. Sunday's work was done.

And the phone hadn't rung again.

All good things.

Padding barefoot through the house, she left her office behind and went in search of a piece of fruit to munch on, trying not to notice the quiet in the house. Both of her siblings had been staying with their families in two of the rented cabins on the property—part of the dude ranch vacation venture she'd started when she'd taken over the place—and the three littles, aged ten and under, had been up at the house with her pretty much anytime she'd been there.

They'd left the day before, all heading back to big-city life, and while all six cabins on the ranch were full of new families having fun, she couldn't help but feel a little lonely.

It took a moment or two to slide her naked toes into her cowboy boots and, peach in hand, she headed outside.

One of the great things about the multifaceted business she'd created out of the once failing Homestead Ranch was that with all of the various ventures going on, there were always people around and things happening.

Which was why the unfamiliar, shiny, new-model green SUV coming up the drive didn't faze her at all. With vacationers on the ranch pretty much all year—including the dude ranch's team building and bonding functions for corporations—the road into what had once been her family's private home was in use pretty much all day every day.

Even when the vehicle turned toward her home, she wasn't concerned. Though the road in was clearly marked—pointing all drivers to keep straight for guests and ranch activities, and designating the right turn for a private residence only—city dwellers new to the property were commonly so taken with the mountain views that they missed the signage.

Figuring she'd grant her newest guests a warm welcome from the owner, she met the vehicle in the circular drive out front of her home, walking up to the driver's door as the SUV slowed to a stop, intending to kindly direct the visitors back to the main road.

As the window rolled down, the genuine smile on her face froze.

Jordon? She had to be imagining…

A quick glance in the vehicle showed her an empty passenger front seat, just as movement in the back drew her attention to double car seats in the back. Filled car seats.

What the…

Eyes piercing sharply enough to hold back the instant spring of emotion that surged through her, Mia pinned Jordon. Looking as though he'd been about to speak, he didn't.

And with another glance directly behind him, neither did she, at first.

How did you cuss out a guy who had no business to be on your property and order him immediately away, with impressionable littles right there within hearing distance?

"You brought your children, Jordon?" Her tone as light as she could make it, she could hardly believe the words she heard coming off her tongue.

In all the years since the man had left Shelter Valley, turning his back on the four years they'd spent as soulmates—and lovers—she'd imagined countless times what she might say to him if ever she saw him again.

Not once had it been the words currently sliding out of her: "Where's their mother?"

Crass, yes. But not overly detrimental to little ears.

Acting as though it had been a week or two since she'd seen their father—not ten years. Trying to sound like she'd been expecting them.

As a good hostess would do.

"I promised the girls they were going to see some horses, and maybe even be able to pet one." The only thing even halfway acceptable about his completely inadequate response was that it was about as inane as hers had been.

"Our mommy's died," a small voice said from the back seat. Followed by, "He didn't say about Mommy when the horse lady asked," in a softer, more familiar tone. One child talking to the other? Mia wondered.

But didn't let herself glance into the back seat another time as horror filled her. Meeting Jordon's gaze, she didn't get a word out.

The lost look in his eyes, accompanied by a silent nod, was all the answer she needed for her heart to start bleeding.

For the motherless children.

Not for him.

And for the mother who'd lost her life so young,

leaving behind such young children…that, too. Most definitely.

"Well then, I think we should make sure you keep your promise and get right down to the horses," she choked out, noting the cringe on his face as she made reference to Jordon's promises.

He most certainly had not kept the one he'd made to her. The part where he'd told her they'd be together forever.

She knew that he'd had to go. That the idea of small-town life suffocated him. Depressed him, even, as it meant he'd have to give up everything he wanted out of life.

Didn't blame him a bit for needing what he needed.

She blamed him for not being honest with her about his dreams or his disdain for Shelter Valley life. She'd made it very clear, before she'd ever gone out with him, that Shelter Valley was her home. That she intended to grow old there.

He'd told her, when it all blew apart, that he thought she'd change her mind. Because her older siblings had hightailed it out of town at their first opportunity.

"Follow me down," she said into the silence that had fallen, unable to breathe freely in air thick with recrimination. And without another glance at any of the SUV's occupants, she started a brisk walk back to the vee in the road and took the straight section of road toward the barns, leaving him to drive at a snail's pace with her back end, straight shoulders and head held high directly in front of him. If he wanted his children to see her horses, he'd follow her. If not, he'd at least have to stay behind her long enough to get back to the main road.

Either that or run her over. She wasn't moving aside.

Not again.

Not for him.

Chapter Two

"Are we going to see the horses now?"

"How long until we get there?"

Reeling from the extremely unwelcome vibes he'd just gotten from his one-time soulmate, Jordon tempered his tone with kindness and answered just as he had the thirty or more other times he'd gotten the question since leaving Phoenix a little over an hour before. "We're on our way to see the horses," he said, and followed with, "we'll be there in a few minutes."

This time, he offered up a prayer that the girls actually would get to see horses. Surely Mia didn't hate him so much she'd make a liar out of him in front of four-year-old parentless twins.

The response from the back seat came exactly the same. Again. "How many is a few minutes?"

And he asked, "How high can you count?"

"Thirty!" Both voices came in unison, their *r*'s, their voices in general, still sounding more babyish than grown-up. They continued, in unison, with the count off.

Giving him to the count of thirty to gather himself. To avoid looking at the long bare legs sauntering slowly in front of him from beneath skimpy jean shorts and disappearing into ankle-length cowboy boots.

That butt...

Oh, Lord, what was the matter with him?

He had no right to remember his hands on that backside. Especially not with his cargo in tow.

And his life imploding so rapidly he didn't have a hope in hell of keeping up.

A little more than twenty-four hours before, he'd been in his luxury high-rise apartment in New York, preparing to hire a couple of college graduates for his investment management firm.

Instead, he'd spent the previous night in a hotel room in Phoenix—his hometown—feeling completely disoriented. Trying not to panic.

He had to tell Mia that the four-year-old twins in the back seat of his rental car were biologically hers.

But not in front of them.

While being any kind of parent was as foreign to him as living on Mars, even he understood that little girls shouldn't hear monumental stuff about themselves in third party, so to speak.

Neither could it be a happy time for them to witness Mia's certain shock over the news.

He had no idea where to find a babysitter.

Hadn't realized that when he met the Sierra's Web team at their office that morning—on a Sunday, so not a business day—that the friend who'd had them for the past week would be there. With the girls, and their immediate belongings, waiting in another room in the suite...

When he'd boarded the plane Saturday night, he'd have bet a million to one that he would never meet, let alone take custody of, the twin kids he'd been contacted about the morning before. Kids he'd never even heard of until then.

Thankfully, Mia's walk to the barn wasn't far. And the girls stumbled over a couple of different numbers, corrected each other and then started over.

Because, apparently, that was the rule.

Mess up. Start over.

Not a bad way to walk through life.

Any chance he could convince Mia to buy into it?

As the woman in front of him stopped, he pulled up beside her in front of a barn, pushed the button to shut off the engine and turned to see both girls... staring blankly.

He'd expected excitement. A scrambling to be free of the car seats they'd insisted on buckling themselves into. Luckily, Mariah O'Connell—the child life specialist who'd met with him at Sierra's Web before he'd actually taken physical custody of the twins—had checked their young attempts, deemed them completely correct, and then had proceeded to teach Jordon how to do what the girls had just proven so aptly they didn't need him to do.

If only she'd given him more than a list of emergency Sierra's Web phone numbers and a half hour lecture on what to do after he drove away.

"You guys want to get out and see the horses?" he asked, looking from one set of blue eyes to a set of brown ones in faces that looked exactly the same to him. It happened, he was told. Sometimes fraternal twins looked almost identical.

Both girls shrugged. In unison.

Two against one.

He didn't have a hope of pulling this off.

"Let's at least get out of the car," he said then. But sat there until he was sure they'd agree with him. No way he was going to put them through some kind of tantrum because he was trying to make them do something they didn't want to do.

He could rule the open floor on Wall Street, but he sensed that he had zero authority with the sprites strapped into the back of his rental car.

No one was moving.

Mariah O'Connell had told him that communication was key to something.

"What's wrong?" he blurted before emotional outbursts started happening. He'd seen them in restaurants…dads carrying kids out on their hips due to seemingly irrational bouts of uncontrollable crying.

And these girls…well, Mariah O'Connell and Kelly Chase, the psychiatrist expert who'd also met with him, had given him an earful about their expected emotional adjustments over the next few days.

"We can't unbuckle," Brown Eyes said, her look definitely not happy. But she didn't seem ready to burst into tears, either.

"It's too hard," the other one said.

Ruby and Violet. He knew their names. He just wasn't sure which one was which. So much had happened in a whirlwind of confusion while his mind had been encased in shock-grown cotton.

That had been fertilized with panic.

"And…we can't get out till someone holds our hands at the door." Brown Eyes again. He was beginning to see her as the leader of the two. Not that he put any stock at all in anything he might perceive in his current situation.

He jumped out. Didn't look at Mia. Couldn't.

Yanking open the back door on his side of the vehicle, he pushed the center button—pretty much all he remembered about the lesson that had come on top of so many other life sustaining pieces of information. And Brown Eyes pulled her arms out of the restraints binding her to the back of the seat. One leg was still held by a strap. A much loosened one.

Was he supposed to hold her hand, then?

What about Blue?

Did he walk one around to the other?

With both girls staring at him, he had to make a

decision. Felt like the wrong one could snap the tiny dab of glue holding the world together. Determining that if Brown got excited and ran off to see the horses while he was unbuckling Blue, catastrophe would be more likely, he told her to stay put and shut the door beside her.

By the time he was around to Blue, Brown was standing on the hump on the back middle floor, her hand on the back of Blue's car seat. Pushing his one button with a sure movement, he stood back, holding out both hands, and was almost weak with relief as Blue and Brown trustingly gave him a hand each and held on to him as they jumped down to the dirt ground beneath his feet.

They'd done it. The three of them. Successfully navigated a thing.

For a second there, he felt like he'd ended the day up a million.

Mia tried like hell to exist on anger.

Far better that than heartbreak, which was pretty much what engulfed her when she saw two little hands reach for Jordon's big ones and jump down on her land.

She'd known he'd be a great dad. He just hadn't seen himself that way.

Hadn't trusted himself to get it right, had been her take on the situation. At least that was how she remembered it.

Years passed. People changed.

And memories…got worn around the edges.

Mariah Montford, adopted daughter of the town's leading family, and founder of Forever Friends, came out of the barn door just as Jordon and the girls reached them. She was a gorgeous woman, the perfect combination of her Native American father and Caucasian mother.

"This is Mariah," Mia said, looking at the girls. She had the wherewithal to remember a little game that the woman who had a degree in youth therapy played with her clients. "Mariah Montford. M&M's like the candy!"

Jordon just stood there. And Mia was out of words.

"Who's this?" the horse therapist asked, looking from the girls to Jordon.

And then to Mia.

Which was when Mia realized that she and Jordon were staring at each other—and saying nothing. How did she introduce him? He was obviously leaving it up to her.

And…

"I'm Violet," the tiny brown-eyed blonde said.

"And I'm Ruby." The girl's blue eyes seemed to glow with importance for a second, but the light quickly dimmed as she looked at the ground.

Catching Jordon's gaze as he looked away from the second small child just as Mia did, she couldn't help but raise an eyebrow.

Of concern.

He'd called multiple times. Had tried to tell her. She'd refused to pick up.

Which didn't give him the right to drive into Shelter Valley, onto her land, and invade her life with…

"Our parents died," Violet said then, looking at Mariah. Her speech, the rounded *r*'s, so adorable Mia almost wept.

While Mariah glanced quickly at Jordon.

"Your mommy, you mean?" Mariah asked, kneeling down to face the two girls. The way they gravitated toward the therapist didn't surprise Mia.

Ruby nodded. "Mommy's died," she said.

"She did." Mariah nodded again, a look of such genuine compassion on her face, Mia almost drifted toward the therapist herself. "What does that mean?"

"I dunno." Ruby shrugged.

"She's not here," Violet added.

"And she can't come back," Ruby said, wide-eyed as the two little ones took a step closer to Mariah. The woman's waist-length black braid seemed to glow in the sun, but it was the real peace on her lovely light brown face that got to Mia, and for a second, Mia envied her.

Mariah Montford had lost both of her biological parents when she'd been only a few years older than the twins. Mia, only a few grades ahead of Mariah in school, hadn't known all the details when they were growing up, but she and Mariah had since become close friends. She knew about the horrors Mariah had experienced, an onlooker as her parents were killed on a hijacked plane. The therapist had been saved by pet therapy as a child, right there in Shelter Valley, and after completing her education at the local university, founded and ran the horse therapy division, Forever Friends, of Homestead Ranch.

From her perch in front of the girls, Mariah Montford looked up at Jordon. "You're their father?"

Mia's gaze shot straight to his face. Watched as he paused, looked at her and then nodded. She hadn't realized she'd been holding her breath until she got a little dizzy and sucked in air.

"You're here to see if the girls might respond to horse therapy?" Mariah asked then, standing.

"Ah…yes," Jordon said. "How do I go about that?"

Laughing softly, Mariah said, "You don't. I do. You girls want to come with me and see the horses?" She held out a hand to each of them.

Without even looking at Jordon, they both took the hands proffered to them. "I won't take them out of your sight," Mariah said, pointing toward the door of the barn she'd propped open. "We'll be right in here."

Jordon watched the three head into the barn, the look on his face…devastated.

He was lost. Well and truly.

Unlike anything Mia had ever seen before. Losing his wife. Raising two small daughters alone.

He'd obviously been right to leave Mia. Had met his soulmate someplace else. New York, probably.

She hadn't been so lucky. He'd been her one true love.

Funny how life worked completely wrong sometimes.

"There are other horse therapy programs," she told him, hurting for him. For those precious little girls. And feeling the fissure he'd left in her heart ripping wide open again.

"Mia…"

She shook her head. Was not going to get into it with him. She would not let him see her cry.

Wasn't going to be happy with herself if she dared shed another tear over him.

Or for him.

He stepped no closer, but moved over, blocking her view of the barn. His back to his daughters. "They're yours, too."

The urgency in his tone, the panic in his gaze… they got through to her.

The man had lost his mind.

Grief from the loss of his wife?

Thoughts flew. She had to get him help.

"Remember the Robinsons?"

Robinsons. Had seemed so altruistic. Jordon needed the money. Her part anonymous. She shook her head. Not because she didn't remember, but…

"No, Jordon. She miscarried, remember?" She spoke as though she was addressing one of his daughters. Truly afraid for him.

And going no further. Her mind, her heart…all frozen right there. In the process of helping him.

"They preserved our embryos. And four years ago, Madeline delivered healthy four-year-old twins."

"They're four." She looked toward the barn. Saw

only him. Didn't move to change her view. Couldn't think. Just stared.

"Keith and Madeline were killed in a boating accident last weekend. They'd hired this Phoenix-based national firm of experts in various fields, Sierra's Web, to draw up and then, if need be, execute, their living trust. I had a certified letter from Savannah Compton, the expert lawyer in the firm, yesterday morning. Under the auspices of child services, the girls have been with the family friend who'd been keeping them for the day Keith and Madeline were meant to be gone. It's all been happening with Sierra's Web oversight and intervention, as determined by the living trust..."

His missive had been spilling forth without him even taking a breath. She heard him. Knew what the individual words meant. Couldn't figure out how to apply them in her current reality.

She was home. Where life pretty much happened based on choices she made.

When Jordon's professor had come to him with the story of his friends who couldn't conceive due to egg and sperm incompatibilities, a desperate couple who'd been seeking college students willing to donate...

Jordon had turned them down on the spot. Had told her about it later.

She'd been the one who'd insisted they help the couple. He'd needed the money to stay in school.

She'd found it all kind of romantic. She and Jordon helping another couple have their own family as a precursor to the children they'd have together some day. When they were ready.

And in the meantime…

She'd made the choice.

One that had ended up being in vain.

Over.

Done.

No way…ten years later…

Shaking from the inside out, she said, "There has to be some mistake." It was all too surreal. Couldn't possibly be happening. Not in real life.

She needed a few minutes alone with her horse. Brilliant would calm her enough for Mia to be able to think.

"I thought so, too. Was certain of it right up until this morning when I was shown documentation. Something about having our DNA from before. And…the Robinsons only had one set of donors."

"But after she miscarried…they decided to adopt."

That's what they'd been told.

What Jordon had told her.

She'd never met the couple. Nor had she talked to the professor. Finance classes weren't part of her degree.

"Apparently, they looked into adoption, but Madeline went into a depression after the miscarriage and decided she wasn't ready to have any child. Wasn't sure she'd ever be ready." He glanced behind them, then continued to speak quickly. "Keith decided to keep our embryos in case Madeline changed her mind and wanted to try again…"

Staring, mouth open, she knew there had to be a mistake. As soon as her brain synapses started firing again, she'd find it.

No way what Jordon was telling her made any kind of sense.

Those precious little girls… His information had to be inaccurate.

She'd figure it all out.

And life would right itself once more.

Chapter Three

He had to rein in his own panic.

Looking at Mia, Jordon got that message loud and clear. "Look, I know you're stunned. Me, too. Blindsided. And what in the hell is going on? But…those two little girls…they've lost their parents. They're with a stranger. A man who knows nothing about children and…"

Mia's eyes wide, she stared at him. Took a step sideways to look at the twins standing side by side, silently watching as Mariah Montford pet a horse. The therapist was talking. He could hear her voice, just couldn't make out her words.

Mariah Montford, a therapist and owner at Homestead Ranch, and Mariah O'Connell, a child life specialist at Sierra's Web. It couldn't be coincidence.

Two women with the same name, approaching him the same day, to help with his girls. It meant something.

"Until the twins announced their names here, I wasn't even sure which was which," he said then. Still so strung out by shock he couldn't seem to process as the situation demanded. "Brown Eyes is Violet. Blue is Ruby."

He wasn't going to forget that again.

"What do you know about them?" Mia hadn't taken her gaze from the direction of the girls.

"Violet seems to be the more dominant of the two. Or at least the most outspoken. She always answers first."

"They told you that?"

"No. I just…any time I asked a question…"

"What did Sierra's Web tell you? Or the friend who had them? Or CPS?" Still not looking at him.

"It's all in the car," he said. "And there's stuff about preschoolers and grief and adjustment. The more stability they have right from the start, the better chance that they'll readjust in a healthy manner…"

Stability? Moving to New York with a guy who didn't have the first clue about raising them?

"I didn't know where else to come."

No response.

"I need you, Mia."

Still staring towards the twins…their daughters… Mia shook her head.

His head dropped as his heart sank. "You're saying you won't help me figure this out?"

She didn't answer and when he looked up at her, she was still watching the girls, her eyes flooded with tears.

Blinking firmly, Mia took a deep breath. She'd have plenty of time to emote in the dark of the night, where no one saw or knew.

"I need proof," she said in a voice that sounded cold even to her. And the words, slightly inane. Two things were becoming clear to her. The authorities would not have turned over two four-year-old orphans to a single man without ample checks and balances. Legalities had been followed.

And there was no way the distraught man standing too close to her would have kidnapped the little sisters. He was clearly scared to death of them.

Maybe someday the memory of Jordon Lawrence afraid, out of his element, lacking in confidence, would bring amusement. At the moment, his out-of-character reactions were only bringing confirmation of a tale so tall she couldn't seem to move.

Not forward.

Not back, either.

"What are your plans?" She'd found a place to start.

"I don't have any."

Her gaze swung in his direction. Seriously? Jordon always had a plan. Always.

He looked her straight in the eyes. "They were

bequeathed to me." As though that made everything fall into place.

But it didn't.

Clearly not for him any more than it had for her. Except… "Only to you."

"Savannah, the lawyer I told you about, said that the Robinsons talked about the fact that they didn't want the girls to be split up or have multiple guardians. And…they had no idea who you were."

Her choice. And there was that word again. Her life was shaped by the choices she made every single day. In recent years, she'd adopted the fact as her own personal mantra.

Because it had given her a sense of security.

The feeling that she was fully in charge of her life and where it went.

"How long have you actually had them in your custody?"

"About an hour and a half."

About the time it took to get from Phoenix to Shelter Valley, with a few minutes to spare for the walk to the horse barn.

He'd brought them straight to her.

"You want me to take them?" She couldn't, of course. Because, well…she tried to swallow past the lump in her throat…she'd always wanted to be a mother.

But she was a ranch owner, with many ventures to oversee. A craft influencer. Busy. Busy. Busy.

Those two precious little blondes were her biological daughters? Elation rose up to make her dizzy for a second. And then her mind, her emotions were clouded and murky again.

"I think I need to adopt them out to a good family," Jordon was saying. "It's the only thing that makes sense. But that's a process, and in the meantime, I don't know. I just…came here."

That fissure in her heart split open a bit more. She didn't fight the warmth that seeped out. She would. She'd scoop it up and shove it back inside.

When she had a minute.

"You bring me my children to tell me you're going to give them away?"

"Mariah O'Connell, the child life specialist I met with at Sierra's Web this morning, mentioned your horse therapy program. Apparently, you do great things with little kids, getting them to confide their true feelings to the horses or something, and, well, as soon as she said the name of your ranch, I knew it was an omen. Not because of the therapy, so much, but…it was too much of a coincidence."

"Forever Friends, the horse therapy program, is a private venture owned and run by Mariah Montford. Homestead Ranch gets a percentage of the profits."

"I was told you own some of the horses."

If he wanted to get technical about it… "Yeah."

"And that you work with them."

"With the horses," she specified. "Not the clients." How much more did he know about her?

It wasn't right, him knowing things about her and her knowing nothing about him or his life.

Macy, the gentle mare Mariah Montford was introducing to the girls, raised a hoof and put it back down. Both little ones stepped back. And Mia ached to have an arm around each one of them, reassuring them that Macy wouldn't hurt them.

Not on purpose.

And knew, in that second, that she wasn't going to hurt them, either. Not if she could help it.

Was it best for them if Jordon adopted them out?

Her heart said absolutely not, but what did she know? She'd given away her eggs, anonymously, and moved on.

Ruby and Violet, two little human beings born from something she'd donated, stepped forward again, each reaching out their tiny hands to Macy's lowered neck. Showing a strength to overcome fear. At least that was what Mia saw, filling with hope for them.

"Maybe a few days at the ranch, in horse therapy, is a good first step." She heard the words before they'd completely registered. Almost as if her heart had purposely rushed them through before her brain could try to nix the idea.

"Unless…do you have a place in Phoenix?" He'd grown up there. She'd assumed he was still in New York, but she'd refused to let herself look him up. Maybe he'd moved back.

Her heart jumped at the thought and she issued a swift reprimand. A reminder.

"No. I own a high-rise apartment in Manhattan."

Okay, well, there then. They really were polar opposites.

"Are you married?" Might figure in to future choices made, at some point.

"No. And before you ask, I live alone."

Right. Good to know.

Her mind immediately pushed back on the satisfaction his answer had given her. The state of his love life had no bearing whatsoever on her or their current situation.

Him living in New York was a big issue, though.

"Do you plan to adopt them out from there?"

Mariah was walking Macy slowly around the barn, the girls on the other side of the therapist, matching her step for step.

"I have no idea." Jordon's tone drew Mia's gaze. And she looked at him. Really looked.

Saw the lines at the corners of his eyes. The shadows beneath them. And the confusion within them.

This wasn't a Jordon she knew.

He was in trouble. And he'd run to her.

Bottom line.

Past aside.

"All of my guest cabins are full, but I have plenty of room in the house," she said. "Why don't the three of you stay here? At least for tonight? It'll give us a chance to talk after they get to sleep."

To come up with some tentative, short-term plans. Period.

Anything else they might have had to discuss with each other had all been said.

He nodded. Shook his head. Ran a hand through his hair. "I… I can stay until they're asleep," he said. "Can I impinge on you for overnight? I just…" He broke off, glanced at the girls for a long minute. Shook his head.

"I know I'm asking too much, Mia, and you're busy here, but you know people, have a whole town of friends to pull from…"

He wanted her to find the adoptive family?

To have her own daughters living right there in Shelter Valley where she'd see them every day?

Ready to tell him to think again, she couldn't get the words out.

Wouldn't she rather be able to watch out for them? To know if they ever needed help?

"I had no warning here, no time to make plans to be away, and I have a couple of major trades to make when the bell rings in the morning. I could be back by two at the latest, tomorrow afternoon. The final bell is at four eastern time."

Which was three hours ahead of Arizona.

And he wasn't asking her to find a family for the girls?

"I don't know anyone, let alone someone I trust well enough to babysit while I work, while you probably have a whole pool to pull from…"

Babysitting. He'd been talking about the two of them needing to work and which of them had a better chance of finding someone to watch the girls.

Relief flooded her in such force she actually smiled at him.

"Okay," she said.

"Okay?"

She nodded.

He smiled.

And that fissure inside her leaked a bit more.

He bugged out at bath time. Mia clearly knew how to bathe girls. How to wash long hair without getting soap in the eyes. He did not.

Nor did he know where towels were kept.

And when the twins announced that they wanted to bathe together—with Violet asserting that's what they always did—he had his exit excuse. The room just wasn't big enough for all of them.

He suggested that he head out as the small group was heading down the hall toward the bedroom that had been assigned to the little sisters. They'd been happy to see that they were sharing a big Mommy-and-Daddy bed, not sleeping in two little-kid beds.

No one seemed fazed by his announcement.

"Bye," Violet said as though she'd been told to do so, nudging her sister, who then said, "Bye." Ruby was busy pulling pajamas out of the suitcase he'd just brought in.

With a quick glance at Mia—who nodded briefly

before giving full attention to the four-year-olds un-expectedly in her care—he made his escape.

And didn't feel anywhere near as relieved and free as he'd thought he would as he drove the dark desert highway back to his elegant high-rise hotel in Phoenix. Had it only been twelve hours since he'd left his suite that morning? Seemed like a lifetime ago.

Maybe because he'd been thrown back a lifetime, seeing Mia.

And Brown Eyes and Blue Eyes…Violet and Ruby…wow. What did a guy do with that?

Chapter Four

What Jordon did half an hour down the road was phone Mia. Wasn't surprised when there was no answer. They were probably all still in the bathroom. Which would be followed by a story, Mia had said, and then bedtime.

Had she ever put kids to bed before?

Of course she had. She'd started babysitting when she was twelve.

But what about little girls who'd been suddenly separated from the two people who'd put them to bed most every night of their lives? And then from the friend who'd had them for the past week?

Inconsiderate of him to have rung in, giving Mia more to deal with. Completely understandable that she hadn't answered.

An hour and a half later, sitting on the couch in his suite in Phoenix with a shot of whiskey in a tall glass filled with water, Jordon looked out of the wall of windows in front of him, overlooking the city that had somehow grown to be the fifth largest in the country since he'd grown up there.

He should be feeling validated. He'd left the desert behind to head to New York City with nothing but the clothes on his back and a prestigious college degree, and ten years later he was back, sitting on the top of the world.

He'd thought about driving by the small house his mother had raised him in after his father had died. Just to remind him how successfully he'd fulfilled his promises to himself.

There'd been no time that morning. Absolutely none, since he'd had two four-year-olds in tow. And after dark...the old neighborhood hadn't called out to him at all. He'd said all he had to say to the space the day he'd moved his mother out of the house and into the lovely waterfront condominium he'd purchased for her in Connecticut.

Another promise fulfilled.

So many of them.

And yet...they still didn't seem to make up for the one promise he hadn't kept.

To Mia Jones.

He'd been so certain that as soon as they'd finished college together and saw the writing on the wall where the failing family ranch was concerned, she'd need more than the small college town where she'd grown up. Where they'd met. That she'd be ready to leave with him—just as her siblings had left town before her.

Shelter Valley was a great, friendly, welcoming place for a college kid to spend four memorable years. But for a financier needing to make his place in the world? He'd have suffocated within a month.

And Phoenix, the state's largest city…hadn't even been a blip on anyone's radar back then. Except with retirees who'd fly in for the winter months, golf until spring and then head back home. At least it had seemed that way to him.

In reality, the city had already grown into an entity, attracting corporate offices to the year-round sunny climate. But no way had he seen what was coming. A metropolis that had tripled in size in a ten-year span.

Not that such insight would have changed his mind. The hub of his profession was New York City. Everything in him had cried out to get there as fast as he could. To make his mark among those he'd studied and followed in the market. And to do it with integrity.

And other than Mia, he didn't have a single regret. At thirty-two, he was who he'd wanted to become. He loved his life.

City lights gleamed. Shining with success.

His glass was half-empty and his phone hadn't rung. He didn't love that.

He was temporarily responsible for two orphaned

children and he had no idea if they'd been able to get to sleep in a strange home, cared for by a person they'd only just met.

Their biological mother, yes, but they didn't know that. Probably wouldn't understand even if they'd been told.

But Mia knew.

His gut clamped. Not in a good way.

What in the hell had he done? Delivering a woman's children to her, out of the blue, with no warning, and convincing her to take them for him? At the same time that he was telling her he was going to give them to someone else?

Had he really become so…

Lost?

From the second he'd accepted custody of the twins, he'd been completely engulfed with desperation.

No excuse for dumping on Mia.

What in the hell had he done?

Phone in hand, not wanting to chance waking the kids, he texted her.

I didn't consider your feelings enough. Not in the past. And most definitely not today. I apologize. Do you want me to come get them now, or in the morning?

If the girls were asleep, and no problem to her, it would be best for them to stay in bed. And Ruby and Violet had to come first.

His phone rang.

Mia.

"I'm sorry," he said, picking up on the first full ring.

"You should be. For disregarding my feelings in the past. But not for today. You were hit over the head by something I initiated years ago. It's right that I help."

A sense of familiarity washed over him. He let it.

"You didn't want to donate," she said then. "You thought it could get messy, and you were right. It has."

"I thought you'd struggle…knowing our baby was out there being raised by someone else." Truth. Not anything that was going to help their current situation.

"And it wouldn't have bothered you."

He hadn't thought so. At the moment, he wasn't sure about any of it.

Except, "As it turned out, we helped create two innocent orphans." A dozen hours later and he still couldn't wrap his mind around the morning's revelation.

"They're skittish and hesitant and mostly quiet," he continued. "Except when it comes to Macy. They stumbled over each other trying to get words out first about that half hour they spent with her, remember? And Mariah, too. Naming her Mariah Macy's Mom." Both girls had laughed as first Violet, then Ruby, had called the therapist the name. It was the first time he'd heard them laugh.

And when Mariah had accepted the special title, acting as though she loved it, the girls had taken her at face value. For the rest of the evening they'd used her full title, expecting everyone else to do so as well, correcting them if they didn't, anytime any of them spoke of Mariah.

He'd noticed. "And they ate the cheese pizza I ordered for dinner." He just kept on talking. He'd had the wherewithal to ask them first if they liked pizza and had received nods in response. He also sounded like he was praising himself.

Maybe he had been.

Not a character trait he wanted to own.

He wasn't overly fond of Mia's lack of response, either. Or the silence that was hanging between them—leaving so much unsaid.

"How long did it take you to get them to sleep?"

"Not long. They're good girls, Jordon. Super well behaved. Well raised."

"Back when you were convincing me to donate, you said everything in the Robinsons' surrogate profile made them seem like they'd be great parents." Apparently she'd been right.

"I read them a story—there were several books in the satchel you brought in. I'm assuming their favorites. We need to find out where the remainder of their belongings are…"

"It's on my list of to-dos tomorrow," he told her. "Everything is in a living trust left to the girls, with me as executor and guardian. The house, and everything in it, is just sitting there waiting for something to happen."

"Didn't Madeline and Keith have relatives? Parents? Siblings?"

"There are a couple of siblings, one on each side. Both brothers. And they both left contact information with Sierra's Web, who passed it on to me, but neither have been in touch with the girls since their parents died." All in the folder sitting unopened on the full-size desk behind him. "They're both married. I thought maybe one of them might be a candidate to adopt the girls. They're family. People the girls know."

He'd felt better thinking about the idea sitting in Sierra's Web that morning than he did in his hotel suite.

"Wouldn't you guess that Madeline and Keith would have left them as guardians, if that's what they thought was appropriate for their children? And that they'd have already expressed an interest in taking them if they wanted them? So that Sierra's Web could give you that option?"

If he'd had half his brain cells working, he might have.

"There was a portable sleep machine device in their suitcase with a note to play the sound of waves. And there was a night-light, too. And a baby monitor. As soon as I had everything up and going, and told them it was time for bed, they cuddled up together and that was it. There hasn't been a peep on the monitor, and I've looked in a couple of times, too."

His gut relaxed. Maybe for the first time all day. "Thank you."

"I'm not doing it for you."

A timely reminder. "I know."

"I think, based on their need for immediate stability, they should stay here, at the ranch, while you figure out the future. The horses are a hit. We can keep their focus there for now. I already called Mariah Macy's Mom. She's willing to take them on…"

Whoa. She was moving fast. Too fast.

While he wasn't moving at all.

Except to drop off his biological daughters immediately after taking custody of them. He'd run them to Mia as quickly as he safely could do so.

"They're my responsibility."

"I'm aware of that. Consider me a full-time baby-sitter until you have a chance to make arrangements."

If anyone had any idea how over-the-top relieved he was to hear her offer, they'd think him a loser, for sure.

He wasn't all that fond of himself at the moment.

"They should get to know me, too, since I'm their guardian," he said, with no clear reason why he'd be pushing himself in where he didn't fit.

"If you're giving them up, what good would it do? They'd just have more people to say goodbye to."

Good point.

"I still want to see them." How could he be sure they had everything they needed otherwise? Maybe he'd see something Mia didn't. "So, if that makes you uncomfortable, I can bring them here." Yeah, right. And set up a playpen in the suite's living area?

As if there was one big enough for four-year-olds. Or he'd put them in one if there was.

"You think it's best for Ruby and Violet to be there with you?"

Looking around at the opulence to which he'd grown accustomed, noting not a single thing of interest to a preschooler, he said, "No." And then, "But there's a great children's museum not far from my hotel," he added. "Mariah O'Connell told me about it. I think they'd like it."

"Even if their parents took them there earlier in the summer? Which they might have done."

Good point.

"I have to see them." There. His bottom line. How could he possibly choose a future that suited them best without first figuring out what they most needed?

"I know."

"Will I be welcomed at Homestead Ranch?"

Her immediate silence cut into him.

"I already told you there was room for you to stay," she finally said.

When his tired and overwhelmed being warmed at the thought, he quickly nixed the idea. "I can commute." After bedtime and back before sunrise if need be. And to be clear on his intention, he added, "I'll need to be here in the city to take care of the estate and other details."

Like visiting private adoption agencies?

No way was he going to get the public authorities involved. He'd keep Brown Eyes and Blue Eyes before he'd make them wards of the state.

"If that's it for tonight, I need to go, Jordon."

Thanking her again, so hugely in her debt he'd never be solvent there again, Jordon gave her a quiet "good night" and hung up.

And sat in the near dark alone, sipping his drink, trying not to think about Mia Jones.

Or the fact that she hadn't even tried to get him to change his mind about staying at the ranch.

Hanging up from Jordon, Mia was suddenly swamped with energy. There was so much to do. So little time to get it done. Plans had to be made, her schedule adjusted.

She'd need…things.

Ruby and Violet would never know she was anything except a babysitter, but that didn't mean she could just pretend that they were no more a part of her than any other child for whom she'd ever cared.

She had no rights to them.

And was fairly certain that Jordon would never agree to give her any. He thought her secluded to the point of unhealthy. Or something close to it.

Words from the past came back to haunt her. The things he'd said when she'd made it clear that she wasn't going to leave Shelter Valley.

Didn't seem to matter to him that she'd been giving him the same message, loud and clear, for the four years they'd known each other, two years as exclusive life partners. He'd accused her of running from life. Hiding away. Being afraid to live fully.

All because she hadn't needed to go find her paradise. She'd been living in it her whole life. Some said she was lucky, knowing so completely where she belonged.

Jordon had thought she just didn't know any better.

Not anything she could change.

But she could choose to focus on the immediate. On doing everything she could to help Ruby and Violet through their crisis, and hopefully build a happy memory or two in their psyches to help them glide more successfully into their futures.

She'd been given a gift.

And would be one to the precious little recently orphaned girls who unknowingly carried her genes.

Jordon had let her take photos of the information included in the girls' file. Online, she ordered a grocery delivery from the local store for early morning, including the boxed macaroni and cheese, frozen fish sticks and fresh bananas that the girls loved. Ruby would eat corn. Violet tolerated peas. Mia had canned sweet corn from her own land. Ordered peas.

And the juices the girls liked, in kid-size boxes with straws.

Next, on a different site, she ordered washable paints in various forms, nontoxic glue, water wings and a couple of size four toddler swimsuits. Sizes were easy, taken from the matching clothes the twins had had on. She chose a one-piece. Purple and pink. With unicorns. She'd seen unicorn T-shirts in their suitcase, and one of the books that came with them was about unicorns. Next, she added jeans, four pairs, also in toddler size 4. And then, with a quick quiet check of their tennis shoes, added two jeweled pairs of cowboy boots to go with them. Paying for overnight shipping, she might have scoffed at the possibility of getting anything by the next day, living—as she did—in a small town an hour from anyplace else. But with the huge online retailer having a major warehouse in Phoenix, she pretty much always got her deliveries on time or early.

And then she moved to her craft room. Pulling out Popsicle sticks, Q-tips, bins of embellishments and some canvas, too.

Ruby and Violet's visit with her was time out of time. She couldn't affect their permanent world, or their future, but she could try hard to show them some happiness and fun during the hours they were with her.

Much later, after several more checks on her sleeping houseguests, she finally made herself go to bed—with her door hanging wide. She lay there, eyes open just as fully, staring at the closed door across the hall.

An hour after that, she slid out of bed, moved quietly down the hall to her office, and sent an email to Savannah Compton, the Sierra's Web lawyer whose contact information was all over the paperwork Jordon had had.

The woman represented the Robinsons, not Jordon. The Sierra's Web fee was being paid out of the estate, on behalf of Ruby and Violet.

And Mia needed to know whether or not a DNA test, proving her biological relationship to the girls, would give her any legal rights to visitation with them.

That done, refusing to listen to a heart that still hadn't learned how to shut out Jordon Lawrence, she went to sleep.

Chapter Five

Jordon did not contact any of the private adoption agencies listed on the internet. He didn't even do the search to create the list.

He didn't drive by the Robinsons' home or contact estate sale companies.

He traded stocks. Touched base with the top people who worked with him, saying only that he had unexpected personal business in Phoenix, and would be working remotely for a week or two. And as soon as the final bell rang in New York, he got back into his rented SUV and turned it toward Shelter Valley.

He didn't call first. Didn't want to be told that later would be better. Or have his call ignored. He was responsible for those two little girls, and he had to see for himself that they were either thriving or not.

How he'd know, he didn't have a clue. But he was a quick study. Once the fog cleared, he'd figure it out. In the meantime, he called his mother. They had a standing Tuesday night dinner date and he was going to miss it.

"That's fine, Jordie, thanks for letting me know," Layla Lawrence said when Jordon explained that he was going to miss dinner. She hadn't asked why. And wouldn't. Layla took life as it came. Didn't get worked up about…well…anything.

Not even when he'd bought her the waterfront condo and moved her from poverty in Phoenix to spend the rest of her life in luxury.

She went with the flow.

Had been going with the flow since his father had died.

Jordon had been eight at the time.

"I'm not sure yet when I can reschedule," he told her, honestly regretful to miss the weekly hours with her. With Layla, he could just be. Once a week, he got out of the rat race and semivegetated on his mother's couch while they watched her favorite game shows together. He'd been telling himself for years that he did it for her.

But he'd known for a while that he did it for himself, too.

"No worries," Layla said now. "I know you're busy."

He'd called off before. Several times a year. Whenever there were functions, theater openings,

private museum gatherings that he shouldn't miss.
He'd appreciated her response each and every time.

But in the rented vehicle, on his way to Shelter
Valley, Layla's lack of motherly nosiness frustrated
him.

She'd asked about his day when he'd been a kid.
Asked about homework. Always remembered to follow up. To pick him up. To show up.

Just hadn't ever asked anything for herself.

And in his adult life, never asked anything of him,
either.

But every single time he called, she was there.
Calm as could be.

"I've got a situation, Ma."

"You got trouble?" No alarm. No blame or condem-
nation, either. Just a request for information.

"No."

"Tell me."

"Remember when I couldn't get another loan for
the last semester at Montford?"

"Yes."

"And then I did."

"Yes. You said it was legal." He'd offered. She
hadn't asked. Nor had she requested to know anything else.

At the time, he'd loved her for that.

"It was. I donated sperm."

"Lots of people do. Quite a few med students, so
I've read."

Layla was always quoting what she'd read. He'd

learned to rely on that information. His mother spent most of her time reading. And was select in what voices she'd allow access to her brain. She vetted everything.

"My sperm was used, Ma." A conversation he'd never envisioned having. In a dozen lifetimes. "Along with Mia's eggs."

"Jordon Lawrence, you better not be about to tell me that you got the sweet girl pregnant and then walked out on her."

Jerking back so hard the seat belt chafed the side of his neck, Jordon focused on the road. Stunned. If he'd ever heard that tone from her, it would have to have been before his father's asthma-related death.

"Jordon?" There was clear warning in her tone.

"No, Ma, I didn't get Mia pregnant. We donated embryos. Professor Newgate knew I needed the money. He had a friend. A doctor and his wife, a psychiatrist, who weren't genetically able to conceive. They were looking for candidates to donate eggs and sperm, which she'd then carry. They were offering a full year's tuition. I turned him down, but when I told Mia about it, she was on fire with the idea. I'd get to finish school, and we'd be giving a couple a chance to have a family like the one we were so excited to have someday…"

His own words stopped him, then. Had he been excited about having babies with Mia? Or was that just another lie he'd told her? A pretense he'd played out because he'd thought she'd change her mind?

He'd thought about finding a good nanny in New York, someday. So...yeah...maybe he'd wanted kids with her.

When he'd been too young to know better.

You couldn't be gone fifteen hours a day and be a good dad.

"What's going on, Jordon?" There was still more than just calm in his mother's tone.

"Mia and I were told the couple miscarried. But they froze our embryos. Tried again, and four years ago they gave birth to twins."

Silence filled the car. Where was Layla's steady offering of "okay"?

"The couple passed away a week ago, Ma. And left the twins to me."

"You have them? Right now? At your apartment?" Staccato.

"No."

And he wasn't going to have them. Or might not. "I shouldn't have said anything," he said then.

"Of course you should have. Where are these children?"

"With Mia."

"Where are you?"

"On my way to Shelter Valley."

"You're in Phoenix?"

"Yeah."

"How's the weather?"

Seriously. "Sunny. Hot. Exactly like you'd expect for mid-August."

"Good. I miss the sunshine. And the heat, too."

She'd never said so.

"What are their names?"

Brown Eyes and Blue Eyes. "Violet and Ruby."

"They're girls." Still something in her voice. It sounded good, whatever it was.

"Yes."

"Am I selfish to even consider keeping them, Ma? Bringing them back to New York with me?" As soon as he heard the words, he berated himself for saying them. Talking like such a thing was a possibility. Or even remotely on the table.

Beyond that, he couldn't remember the last time he'd asked for her opinion.

Was there anything he could do for her? Anything she wanted? Those were the questions he generally presented to Layla.

Another silence fell, and he waited. As though his mother's advice would solve the whole issue. Layla knew things.

"You're their father, Jordon."

That was it? A statement of a fact he already had?

"Yeah." He needed more.

"You'll figure it out."

"Would you like it if I brought them home?" Was he looking for justification he didn't have? Trying to guilt himself into doing something that didn't seem right?

"This isn't about me, Jordie. My job is to support, not to dictate, the direction in which your life goes.

And your job is to put the welfare of your children first."

"You think I should put them up for adoption."

"I didn't say that."

No, but she hadn't been happy as a single parent. And he hadn't been as happy in a single-parent home as he'd been with two parents.

Grief had played a part in that. But Ruby and Violet were grieving, too. As much as four-year-olds could.

"What does Mia want?"

"She hasn't said. Except to point out that the Robinsons left the girls solely to me for a reason." Or rather, she'd made note of the fact that they'd chosen him over their own siblings. If they'd wanted Ruby and Violet to go to their aunts and uncles, then they'd have appointed them guardians. "They made a conscious choice, Ma. They knew I live in the city. Knew what I do. And they still chose me." Did that mean the Robinsons wanted him to raise their daughters in New York?

His daughters, now, too.

And Mia's, biologically.

"Is she married?"

"She lives alone." He'd been told that much by Sierra's Web, when they'd talked about her horse therapy program. That was when he should have told them that Mia was the girls' biological mother. "But I have no idea if she's involved with anyone. I didn't ask."

He should have.

Hadn't wanted to know.

"Would you help, Ma? If I did bring them home?"

"Yes." That tone was back. The new one. He liked it.

But wasn't sure he was being fair to her, either.

The day hadn't started out all that great—aside from the fact that Mia had woken up for the first time with her own biological children in her home. Ruby woke them all up at six, crying for her mother. Violet's lower lip had been trembling by the time Mia made it across the hall.

Having had the crying preschoolers dress quickly, redirecting Violet to help her grab clean shorts and shirts for both of them, she'd explained to them that Macy was waiting to help them anytime they missed their mom. Crossing her fingers and hoping that she hadn't just created worse problems. Macy wouldn't always be available. She'd said it only because she'd once heard Mariah, now Mariah Macy's Mom, repeat similar words to seven- and eight-year-old siblings who'd lost an older brother in Iraq.

As a distraction, the idea had worked. There'd been no more tears. She'd made cheesy scrambled eggs for breakfast. They'd both eaten some. They'd emptied grocery bags when they'd arrived, placing items on the table as she'd asked.

Her idea to let them see everything, to recognize things they liked, seemed to have worked. She'd heard Violet tell Ruby "macaroni and cheeses" as she'd put them on the table. Ruby, with her hand in her own bag, had nodded and then, pulling out a box of the toaster pastries they liked, had announced them.

When that moment had brought tears to Mia's eyes, she'd quickly diverted herself. To being thankful the twins had each other.

And she had a chance to get to know them, for whatever brief time they were there.

Or…perhaps…for longer.

She'd heard back from Savannah Compton by midmorning. The lawyer had told her that she had every right to file a motion to prove biological maternity of the girls and request visitation. Whether or not the court granted her request the lawyer couldn't say. As the twins' attorney, she'd want an expert opinion from Kelly Chase, also a Sierra's Web partner, as to Mia's suitability in the girls' lives.

During the girls' half hour with Mariah Macy's Mom, Mia had spoken to her own attorney, Jane Sylvester, who'd agreed to file the motion, and she'd scheduled an appointment with Kelly Chase, too, who'd chosen to do at least the first session at the ranch the next day, during the twins' session with Macy. She wanted to see Mia in her own environment.

And, Mia had surmised, and had confirmed through her attorney, to see the girls in that environment, too. If they happened to be there at the time of Kelly's visit.

Under Jane's advice, Mia had opted not to tell Jordon about the motion. Jane figured that Savannah would tell him at some point, as he was the girls' guardian, but probably not until the motion had been filed.

Sierra's Web, including Kelly Chase, were already employed on the girls' behalf. Seeing them at the ranch was within Kelly's jurisdiction.

The thoroughness with which Madeline and Keith had provided for their daughters in the event of their deaths spoke a whole lot about how much the couple had adored the girls.

And Mia adored them for it.

"Hey...hey, you..." Mia glanced over as she realized the little girl voice had been trying to get her attention. Sitting at the smaller craft table she'd set up for them, the twins, making houses out of glue and cotton swabs, had been talking to each other in words Mia was still struggling to decipher, and Mia's mind had wandered.

"That's not powite, Viyet," Ruby leaned over to whisper loudly at her sister's shoulder. "'Member...'" Ruby's words drifted off on one that Mia understood—remember.

"It's okay," she jumped in before things could go south again. "I'm Miss Jones, like Jordon told you, but my first name's Mia. It's easier. You can call me that."

"Mia!" Violet's giggles stopped Mia in her tracks. The childish sound, the purity, took any breath she had. And…why was her name so funny?

Jumping up from the table, Ruby started to wiggle her hips back and forth. "Mama Mia…" was all she got out before Violet had joined her, moving her own hips as both girls yelled out their rendition of one of the choruses of the popular show tune.

And then repeated it a second time. Putting the most emphasis on the Mama Mia part.

She couldn't help the grin that split her face. The joy on those faces…

The cuteness overload in the dancing.

Their parents had taught them show tunes.

And…

"I'm calling you Mama Mia," Violet announced.

"Me, too," Ruby said.

And Mia, her heart choking her, glanced up to see Jordon entering the room.

"Hey, girls, whatcha making?" he asked, kneeling down to inspect the half-built, slightly tilted houses.

With more of their normal reticence, the twins explained, in their own words, the project they were working on. Finishing sentences for each other.

If Jordon noticed the sudden lack of joy in their polite conversation, he gave no indication of it to them. He praised their efforts. Made suggestions.

Helped right a wall that was on the brink of falling down.

There was no doubt that he was glad to see the girls doing well.

But the look he sent Mia, the sharp ping it sent through her, left no doubt that with her, he was not at all pleased.

Chapter Six

"You told them you're their mother?" Frayed around the edges, Jordon shot the question at Mia the first second they were alone.

Standing in the craft room, listening to the girls chatter in the bathroom down the hall as they washed glue off their hands, he shook his head.

As if they weren't all dealing with enough...

How was he going to explain...or take them with him...

What had she been thinking?

A few seconds passed before he realized that Mia wasn't answering him.

And when she did, her eyes on fire, she said, "Don't ever come into my house again without knocking first."

"I did knock. Several times." And had wanted to check the house before heading down to the barns. Because he'd look really out of place if his charges weren't there.

"You could have called my cell..."

Right. He hadn't thought that far. "You have a habit of not answering," he said, inanely. As though the fact had played a part in the way he'd opened Mia's front door and walked through her house as though he belonged there.

Had every right to do so.

"Ruby and Violet are your wards. I will always answer my phone to your call when they are with me."

Good to know.

Very good to know.

And she still hadn't responded to his initial charge.

Why would she...didn't seem right to do that to little kids who didn't really even get the concept of death yet...talking about biology and...

He stared at Mia. She stared back.

"You...didn't tell them." He read the truth in her eyes before he let it resonate from within. Of course she hadn't. She wouldn't.

"No. I said they could call me Mia. Apparently their parents were show tune folks, or at least one of them was. They were singing it, and dancing, right before you came in."

He'd heard the giggles. They'd rent through him, pushing him toward the sound, lighting him up in a way that scared him to death.

"I'm sorry."

"You should be."

With a grimace, he nodded. "I really do have a lot of good qualities," he told her then. Contrary to what he'd shown her.

"I know you do, Jordon. I wouldn't have loved you, otherwise."

Another kick in the gut, though he was fairly certain that Mia didn't know those words would hurt.

"Do you object to them calling me Mama Mia?"

Yeah. He did. Because it hit him low.

He was a guardian. He didn't come first. "Absolutely not," he told her, giving her the other truth. "They made a choice. And it seems to make them happy." He smiled.

She smiled back.

Ruby appeared, her upheld hands dripping water down to her elbows and then to the floor. "Viyet got water on the floor!" she said, her *r*'s sounding more like *w*'s.

And Jordon wanted to laugh out loud.

Needing Jordon out of her house—at least for a minute or two so she could wall off her heart to his presence—Mia suggested a trip down to the barn to visit with Macy. Clearly, she had to figure out a set of guidelines that would give him as much time with the girls as he required, but not in her home.

Seeing him suddenly appear in her craft room,

looking all important in his dress pants, shirt and tie, and shiny black shoes…she didn't need that.

The memories she was making with her daughters were extremely precious. And private. She didn't want them tainted with the Jordon heartache that had been plaguing her since the day he'd driven out of town.

She'd already reserved a cabin for him. It was one of the two-bedrooms, both with queen beds, so the girls could sleep together. And if he still chose to commute, he could use the cabin for his time with them. Unfortunately, it wouldn't be available until Saturday…

They were only a few steps on their way from the house when a car drove past, sending a wave of dust that didn't matter to her always-dusty cowboy boots, or make a difference to the tennis shoes the girls had been wearing all day, but it definitely coated Jordon's expensive-looking dress shoes.

She wasn't sorry.

About the dust.

He didn't belong in Shelter Valley.

"You have cabins." He nodded toward the turn-off the car had taken as the twins skipped ahead of them a couple of feet. She loved that they already knew their way.

And that they felt comfortable enough to head off on their own.

Keeping her gaze firmly on the girls, she answered Jordon. "Six of them. My dad had a life-insurance policy and I used my portion of the money to start a dude ranch the year after he died. It's busy year-round." There. Now that felt good. Letting him know that he wasn't the only one who knew how to make a buck.

"Race you!" Ruby called to Violet and started running at full speed. Violet, a second behind, took off after her sister, got tangled up in her own feet and face-planted in the dust. Hard.

Heart in her throat, Mia rushed forward, reaching the little girl—her daughter—at the same time as Jordon did. She lifted Violet to her feet, getting a quick look at skinned knees, a similar mark on the four-year-old's chin, no profuse bleeding, and picking her up, cradled the sobbing child to her chest.

"What's wrong with Viyet?" Ruby was back in a flash, and Jordon lifted her up. Glanced at Mia over the girls' heads.

"She's fine," Mia told Ruby, the compassion in her tone coming as naturally as if she'd known the girls their whole lives. "Just a little scraped."

Her brown eyes brimming with tears, Violet pulled back enough to look down at her knees and then started crying again. "I'm bleeding!" she wailed.

At which point Ruby scrambled to get down and moved over to inspect. "It's not dwipping, Viyet," she said, sounding more like a mom than a kid in that second.

"It's not?" Violet looked down again. She gave a

dramatic dry sob and squirmed to get down. "I want Mommy," she said.

"Mommy's goned." Ruby sounded like she might cry, too.

Mia knelt down to the two girls. "Mommy's gone, but you two aren't alone," she said. "You have a lot of people who love you and will take care of you. And you have each other!"

"I was really hoping you were going to introduce me to Macy," Jordon added, also down on his haunches.

Mia glanced over at him, met his gaze for the second she allowed hers to remain connected to his. And felt as though she might cry, too.

For a second there, he was just as she had so long ago envisioned he'd be in their future together.

The future he'd abandoned.

And just as the twins' mommy was "goned," so was all faith Mia had had in any future for her and Jordon Lawrence.

He wasn't the devil. Wasn't a bad guy.

He was just too different from her and she was too different from him, for them to build a life together.

For her own sake, and also for their girls' future stability, that was a fact Mia couldn't afford to forget. Even for a second of eye contact.

Jordon stayed until after bath time. While Violet's knees were more pink than actually scraped, he put salve on them for her. And a dab under her chin, too.

Sitting on the end of their bed, he read a story to them, turning the book around so the girls could see it. "Like watching TV," Violet had said.

And then, turning on the sound machine and baby monitor as Mia had explained, he wished them sweet dreams, closed their door and went out to find Mia.

She wasn't in the living room, kitchen or craft room. He couldn't just leave without letting her know the girls were alone.

Remembering his misnomer from earlier, he pulled out his phone. Texted her.

She was outside on the porch. Having half a glass of wine. The baby monitor on the gently rocking swing beside her.

While he hadn't been overly fond of spending time at the seeming-to-be-falling-down ranch when he'd been in town attending Montford, he'd always had a fondness for that porch. Made of wood, painted white, with picket railings, it had seemed to represent easier times. Bygone eras where families were large and people laughed a lot.

A much too fanciful thought for a guy like him.

"The salve was a good call, thank you," he said, as he sat on the edge of one of a pair of large, cushioned wooden porch chairs.

Wineglass held in both hands, she nodded. Seemingly more interested in a truck coming up her drive than in him, his gratitude or any communication between them.

"You expecting someone?"

For all he knew, she could have a date. She was young. Successful. Beautiful.

Savvy, compassionate, fair…

Shaking his head, he got his mind back on track as she said, "No. That's a retired couple from Phoenix who are renting a cabin here for a week while their house is being partially remodeled. He grew up on a farm in Iowa and thought the dude ranch sounded like fun."

He was happy for them. For her success. It wasn't what he'd wanted to know.

"Are you seeing anyone?" He was more direct the second time out. "Someone who's going to be affected by the girls being here?" It was only for a few days.

For horse therapy.

While he sorted things out.

"No." No what? She wasn't involved with anyone? Or she was but he wouldn't be affected by the girls staying with her?

As her glance passed over him, like he was a stranger in line in front of her, he accepted her answer as it stood and moved on.

"Outside of my life in New York, I didn't make any calls today," he told her. "Not to deal with the estate, the house or anything to do with the girls."

He had their medical records. Their current pediatrician's address and phone number. The password to their patient portals. Hadn't even looked at them yet.

He'd been told the girls were healthy and up-to-date on all inoculations.

"There's no rush on my account."

That was good to know. He wanted more from her. Didn't know what.

But he was pretty sure it was more than he had a right to ask. More than she'd be willing to give.

He couldn't go back.

And even if he could, he wouldn't choose differently. Other than to be more up-front with Mia, earlier in their relationship, about needing out of Shelter Valley.

"I can hire someone to clear out the house, have an estate sale, but, obviously, I need to go in and clean out anything that appears personal or might be meaningful to the girls, now or in the future."

When he paused, and she didn't comment, he continued, "Mariah O'Connell, the Sierra's Web child life specialist, told me that since the girls haven't asked to go home, it might be best not to risk setting them back in their moving-on process by taking them to the house they shared with their parents. But she said that there's no real way of knowing if it would hurt or help, and that, ultimately, the choice is up to me."

"What are you going to do?"

The question was a turning point for him. The Mia he'd known and loved, the woman who'd talked him into donating embryos in the first place, would have spilled every thought she had on the matter.

She'd never had a problem putting her opinions into the mix.

"I don't know," he told her. But didn't ask for any more from her, either.

And she didn't give him any more.

Except a quiet good-night, when he stood up to leave.

She was back in her house, the lock secured behind her before he made it down the porch steps.

Chapter Seven

The girls loved their jeans. The package had been dropped on the porch after Jordon left the night before and, hoping for a happier start to the twins' second morning waking up in her home, she'd entered their room at the first sound of stirring, with denim-draped arms and a pair of tiny cowboy boots in each hand.

Her biological daughters had scrambled over each other to get to her.

"Look, Wuby, pwetty jewels!" Violet's little voice had flooded Mia's heart as the brown-eyed blonde glanced at the jeans. But the moment was brief.

The boots had stolen the morning. The girls had insisted on having them on their feet before they'd get off the bed. And had worn them with their nightgowns to breakfast.

She showed pictures of the event to Kelly Chase later that morning as they started their session. Mia had made solar tea with fresh orange slices and invited the woman to sit at the table where the photos had been taken.

She wanted Kelly to see her as she really was because while she loved her life and thought she could bless the twins' lives, her perspective was only her own.

Maybe their new start would work better without her interference. She could certainly see how less complicated would be best.

And told the psychiatrist so, before the woman had even asked her first question.

"Relax," Dr. Chase said, her blue eyes kind. Around the same age as Mia and blonde like her, Kelly's hair was loosely curled and hung midway down her back. Unlike Mia's messy, short-layered mop. "You aren't on trial here."

"Both your expert attorney, Savannah Compton, and my own attorney here in town said that you'll be an expert witness, testifying before the court, on my motion to have visitation with Ruby and Violet." She couldn't say my daughters. Not out loud.

No matter how loudly her heart was crying out for them.

She hadn't birthed them.

To the contrary, she'd given them away at the embryo stage without looking back.

"That's right, but by opinion isn't based on your

answers to specific questions. It's based on my assessment of you."

Didn't make her feel any better. If anything, being on trial with no direction to follow was worse. "Can I ask you a question then?"

"As many as you'd like." The woman's smile, the seeming compassion in her voice, helped. A tad.

A very small tad.

"This is so different from having become pregnant and finding myself unable to care for a child in the best way possible, which is what any of these cases I looked up last had to do with. I wasn't faced with anything unexpected. I actually created embryos with the express purpose of giving them away. For money. Which makes me seem less than...worthy to have any rights to these children. Do you honestly think I even have a chance?"

She was going to try. The motion was already being filed.

But...should she get her hopes up at all?

Taking a sip of tea, Kelly—as the psychiatrist had asked to be called—seemed to be giving the question careful consideration. This oddly calmed Mia.

"I've never heard of a situation like this, either," Kelly finally said. "And I did some looking, too. There are many instances where a woman donates eggs, but your situation with Jordon...it's unusual."

Unusual to the point of hopeless?

Heart pumping, Mia wanted sunshine and warmth. She wanted to be outside. Surrounded by the mountains she'd scaled—reminding herself that she was strong and capable.

She wanted to close her eyes and breathe in the desert air that had always sustained her.

No amount of self-control, discipline or will was going to help her change a choice she'd made so many years before.

"You didn't even meet the Robinsons," Kelly further pointed out the facts against her, and Mia almost stopped her. Wanted to tell the psychiatrist she no longer wanted the answer to her question.

"I read their surrogate file." The words were burning so hot inside her she had to give them release. "Every word. Several times. I gave Jordon a list of questions to pose to them. I still have the list, and their answers, if that will help."

Brows raised, Kelly cocked her head for a second and said, "That would be very helpful."

Mia jumped up and went to retrieve the paperwork from her nightstand drawer. She'd been obsessing over the file she'd made ten years before, but didn't want it out where the girls might see it.

Not that they could read...

Kelly took the file. Placed it on the table to the left of her elbow. Waited for Mia to sit back down, before resting her arms on the table, leaning in. "What you did, giving an infertile couple a chance to birth their own child, was altruistic," she said, and Mia's blood started running hard in the other direction. "And you didn't do it for the money for yourself. Jordon told

us on Sunday that you did it so that he could afford
to finish his last year of college."

"That's right."

"Those facts will carry weight with the judge."

Mia blinked. Tried to take a deep breath. "You're
telling me you think I have a chance?"

Kelly nodded. "The fact that the Robinsons chose
to leave their children to a biological parent can't be
ignored. They chose Jordon Lawrence, but according to Savannah, they never knew your name, so you
couldn't be a consideration."

"I...at the time... I didn't want anything from
them. I didn't want to be a face, or a person, to Madeline. I wanted her to be the only mother of her babies."

When Kelly just watched her, Mia blurted, "That
sounds like I didn't want them, I know, and here I
am saying I want rights, but if the Robinsons were
still alive, I wouldn't be asking. It's just...knowing
they're orphaned..."

"And having met them..."

Oh, God. Having met them. She'd never been so in
love with anyone in her life. And she'd only known
them two days.

"Jordon and I were engaged. I thought we'd have
our own children when we were ready..."

And here they were...with their children...and
they were never going to be ready to parent them as
the partners she'd once envisioned.

"He thinks I run from life. That I hide away here

in Shelter Valley so I don't have to take risks, and that I'm essentially wasting my life by not finding out how much more there could be."

"What do you think?"

"That I've taken more risks right here on this ranch than I'd ever have taken anywhere else. That I've built something that fulfills me to my core. I rent out the tillable acreage for half the profits. I used every dime of my share of my father's life insurance to build the cabins, buy horses and cows, to hire help, and now have a dude ranch that sustains the ranch all on its own. And, on the side, I've become a crafting influencer, reaching millions of people all over the world, and all I set out to do there was share my ideas with other crafters and hopefully have them share back." Hearing herself, she stopped abruptly.

She sounded like some kind of self-absorbed twit.

"I…uh…did what I said I was going to do when I majored in business," she finished, much less passionately. "I turned my family's failing homestead around and made it profitable again so that not only can we gather here, but our children will grow up knowing their legacy as well."

"I understood that you own the ranch alone," Kelly said.

"I do. I bought my brother and sister out of their shares, but they come home every chance they get now. I've got two nieces and a nephew, all ten and under, who have their own horses in the barn."

The plug was intentional. If Ruby and Violet were

allowed to visit, they'd have biological cousins and aunts and uncles in their lives. But the point she'd started with mattered.

She was a person who did what she said she was going to do. Which meant the girls could count on her.

And Jordon, or whatever family he gave them to, could count on her to not overstep her boundaries, too. Because she made sure her attorney put that in her argument before the court.

"You talk about the dude ranch, the crafting, the actual farming of land, but you didn't mention Forever Friends."

"It's not my program. I had nothing to do with starting it, and I have nothing to do with running it," she said.

"I'm aware of Mariah Montford's work," Kelly said then. "I sent a couple of teenagers her way recently," the psychiatrist continued.

Mia wanted to know who. And how they'd done. But knew the doctor worked under confidentiality laws that wouldn't let her say more.

"McKenna Meredith speaks highly of you and what you've done with this place. She's the one who told me about Forever Friends."

She knew who McKenna was, of course. Her dad and half brothers owned the local construction company. And after the shooting up at her dad's place, everyone in town knew of her.

She hadn't realized McKenna knew enough about

her to tell anyone anything. "She's a year younger than me," Mia said aloud. "I graduated high school the year before she moved here to live with her father. And she only moved back a month or so ago." The expert bodyguard had not only been the talk of Shelter Valley, but she'd been on national news, too, when she'd risked her life and helped expose a killer who'd framed a man for one of the country's most recent white-collar crime sprees.

Beyond that, McKenna came from old money in Phoenix, not like the new fortune Jordon had built, but she'd just chosen to take a lead training position with Sierra's Web, was getting married and settling right there in town. Or rather, in one of the lovely homes her family's company was building up on the mountain overlooking Shelter Valley.

Her fiancé, a one-time corporate accountant, had money, too. New money like Jordon's. He'd just opened an accounting firm in town.

"She's been with Sierra's Web for years," Kelly said. "We're very lucky she chose to stay with us and head up our bodyguard experts. We'd have sorely missed her talents."

Okay, then. Sierra's Web loved McKenna. And McKenna, who had clout, spoke highly of Mia. That had to be good, didn't it?

"I'm hoping it also stands in my favor that Jordon brought the twins to me," she said then, getting in another one of the points she'd had firmly in mind for that morning's critical meeting.

"Speaking of which have you told him yet that you're filing the motion?"

"No." The girls' lawyer would tell him. Because he was their guardian. He'd have ample time to get his own lawyer. "I thought it would be better to keep it all in the courts. It's not personal and I don't want it to become that way. Besides, I'm not fighting Jordon's custody." She just wanted established legal rights of her own.

In case Jordon decided to cut her out again.

"It might be better coming from you." Kelly's words were soft, but firm, too.

"Better in the eyes of the court?" That's what mattered. If she got rights, she and Jordon could work something out professionally. Amicably.

Just like they were with her babysitting in the interim.

"Better for the girls." Kelly's words stopped Mia's thoughts. "If you and Jordon can't talk about something as important as this, how are you going to be able to make other choices? Beyond that, children sense tension between adults. And I'd guess that Jordon would feel a bit blindsided if he doesn't get this from you."

Right. She hadn't considered Jordon's feelings. Because…well, they were off the table for her. But when his feelings would affect the girls…

"I should have thought of that. If it's not inappropriate for you to ask Savannah to hold off talking to him about it until I have a chance to tell him,

I'll do so as soon as possible. I can text you as soon as it's done."

The other woman agreed to Mia's plan. And seemed pleased by the house and the part of the ranch she toured during her visit as well. By the time Kelly's car was pulling off Homestead Ranch, Mia was actually allowing herself to think of a future that didn't involve being forced to say to goodbye to her little girls forever.

Jordon was just sitting down to the lunch he'd ordered delivered to his suite when his phone pinged a text message.

The final bell had rung in New York ten minutes before. He'd signed off from all work sessions for the day.

Unless someone had a problem…

Grabbing his phone, he dropped his fork when he saw Mia's name on the screen.

If you're going to the house today, or when you do, you should make sure to get all photos, including framed ones on the walls or on furniture. Most particularly any including Madeline, Keith and or the girls.

For a second there, he felt a bit more like himself. The opinion he'd been seeking the night before, the one his ex-fiancée had refused to give, had just come through.

Will do, he quickly texted back, then grabbed his

fork and took a huge bite of the grilled chicken salad
he'd specifically chosen because if work had run over
and lunch had to wait, the salad would fare better
than a hot sandwich would have done.

Also, as many of their clothes as you can gather.
And anything that sits on their beds—special pil-
lows or stuffed toys. And check for bath toys, too.

He sent back a thumbs-up, keeping it cool, but
had more of an appetite than he'd had since Sunday morning.

Mia was coming around.

That mattered.

And he had a specific purpose for his day—a way
to help his new charges that was clear and in the moment. Instead of calling the numbers Sierra's Web
had given him for help cleaning out the Robinsons'
home, or meeting candidates at the house for interviews, he spent the afternoon in the home alone.

With the boxes he'd picked up on the way.

And was feeling pretty damned good about himself, about life, when he pulled into Homestead
Ranch just before dark that evening. He'd texted Mia
to let her know he'd be missing dinner.

And why.

The girls had had macaroni and cheese, she'd
texted back. And suggested that maybe he wait
and bring the girls' things into the house after they

went to sleep. So they didn't get worked up—good or bad—right before bedtime.

He'd already had the thought, though he didn't say so. More, he wanted Mia to go through things with him, in case he'd included something that might cause a trigger he hadn't thought of. He'd read and reread the report from the child life specialist and was certain Mia had as well.

But ultimately, every child was different, and there was no guaranteed best way to handle any of the things facing the girls in the present and near future.

He liked not having to carry the weight of that reality all on his own. Felt better equipped to take up the reins of responsibility and start thinking about next steps for Ruby and Violet.

He liked having Mia in his life again.

Chapter Eight

Kelly's input had sent Mia into an emotional quagmire. For her own mental health, she had to keep all feelings for Jordon Lawrence firmly under lock and key. They were a disease to her. Didn't serve her life's purpose or her happiness.

But she needed to work with him, not apart from him, to keep tensions between them minimal for the girls' sakes.

Even though she and Jordon weren't and never would be together again, they had to work together when it came to Ruby and Violet.

She'd do it. Even if it didn't serve her.

But she'd be a better part of the girls' lives if she could find a way to work with Jordon and remain emotionally detached.

Problem was, she had no time to figure out exactly how she went about doing that before he showed up at the ranch that evening, looking all gorgeous and familiar to her with the warm glow in his blue eyes, blond hair a bit ruffled. Even the dress pants, shirt and shoes—far different from the shorts and jeans she'd seen him in pretty much every day during the four years they'd been together—didn't seem to distance him from her.

Sending the texts had been a good first step.

The second one was going to be a lot more difficult. A potential land mine.

Because she got the girls all day, and he was their legal guardian and therefore the biggest entity in their lives, she did as she had the night before, and left him alone to handle bath time, an hour of evening play and story time.

She didn't get to tell them good-night, or tuck them in.

She wasn't petitioning the courts to allow her to do so.

For a few days, she was being given the blessing of starting their days with them, though. Seeing their sweet morning smiles, hearing the innocent chatter as they ate breakfast, brushed their teeth and she got them dressed for the day.

Helping them make their bed—just because she'd learned young and thought it a good practice.

Whether or not Jordon was piling up memories of his time with the twins, like she was, she had no idea.

Just as, when he came out to join her, baby monitor in hand, she didn't ask if he'd contacted adoption agencies that day.

Still in her jean shorts, tank top and cowboy boots—her everyday ranch attire—she helped him carry in the boxes he'd packed up, stacking them all in what used to be her brother's bedroom at the end of the hall, and was currently furnished as generic guest space. A room the girls had peeked in once and shown no interest in since.

And then, as he opened the first box, she said, "I'm petitioning the court to prove that I am the girls' biological mother, and to then be granted visitation rights." It had seemed right in her head, just putting it on the table between them like anything else they should discuss.

The way his mouth fell open—and his gaze shut to her—told her she might have made a mistake.

For the girls' sakes. Only for them.

There was nothing else between Mia and Jordon. Not friendship. Not anything except the ten years of complete silence that had existed between them until he'd called and shown up at her door on Sunday.

Trying to figure out why he looked like he'd just been slapped, she figured maybe she could have thought things through better. Thought of her words from his perspective.

Even a stranger deserved that much.

While thoughts flew, she came out with the first one that presented itself the most clearly. "I'm not intending to interfere with any choices you make for them." But she should have seen that it could look that way.

When he looked over at her, seeming to be listening, she stood inches from the box top he held with both hands and said, "I fully respect your rights as their guardian, Jordon, and whatever you choose, whatever family you choose for them, is your choice. I'm just asking for the right to see them, as regularly as possible, as they grow up. If you adopt them out in New York, that won't be all that often, but it will still be regular. Something they can count on."

She felt like she was babbling. And stopped for a moment.

She didn't owe him anything.

And if the courts deemed it so, she deserved what she was asking for. She certainly deserved the chance to try.

She continued, "I can see where it might make the adoption a bit harder, to ask a family to accept permanent visitation to their children from a stranger to them, but if the court determines that it's in the girls' best interest to know me, then I have to be there for them in whatever way I can be."

Because she loved them more than her own life.

She didn't owe him that information.

"I made a choice ten years ago that ultimately made two helpless and precious little girls orphans," she said, instead.

When he still said nothing, something else occurred to her. "I'm not trying to pressure you to stay in their lives," she added. "I pressured you into donating to the Robinsons, Jordon. I know that. I acknowledge it, fully. This is on me."

"I wasn't under duress when I provided my sperm."

No. In the end, he'd said he was glad they'd done what they did. And not just because it let him finish school.

That mattered. More in the current situation than it had in the past. "It felt good, didn't it? Helping another couple have the family they'd always wanted."

He finally met her gaze.

Nodded.

And told her good-night.

Five minutes down the road, Jordon considered turning back. He'd handled the situation like the somewhat self-righteous ass he'd been ten years before when he'd figured he knew the right answers so well that Mia would figure them out and change her mind about leaving Shelter Valley.

He might not have entered the highway back to Phoenix if not for the fact that he wasn't feeling much more mature than he had back then.

He texted her, though, through the vehicle's voice controls. Asking her to please not go through the boxes he'd packed without him.

More of his lesser self coming through, he was sure. He already knew what she'd find in those boxes.

Had touched every item himself, putting them in the boxes.

And yet, he wanted to go through them with her. To discuss what was best for the girls to have immediately, and what to hold back.

Ten minutes down the road, he called her.

She'd said as long as she had the girls, she'd answer.

And she did. On the second ring.

"I don't appreciate that you filed a motion with the courts before talking to me," he put it right out there. "I'd have given you the rights, Mia. By God, you have to know that, at least. I brought them straight to you the second I got them!"

And she didn't trust him enough to...

Yeah, that stung.

Like hell.

"If you adopt them out, you won't have a say in what rights I have," she calmly pointed out.

"So...you can't go to court when that necessity arises?"

"If I haven't already established my rights, made them a part of the adoption, my chances of getting them dwindle. The adoptive parents could have a say, as legally, at that point, the twins are fully theirs."

He hadn't thought that far ahead.

She had.

Didn't make him feel any better.

"You don't trust me."

"Not to make choices on my behalf, I don't."

He hadn't thought the wrench in his gut could twist any further. It did.

Funny thing was, he didn't blame her.

"I'm sorry."

"I know."

"But it doesn't change anything, does it?"

"We are who we are, Jordon. That hasn't changed."

Did it make any difference that he wanted it to have done so? While he was trying to find a palatable response to his silent question, her voice came softly over the car's speaker system again.

"Ultimately, no matter who you are or what did or didn't happen between us, I would still be filing this motion. You've got legal rights, but what if something happened to you before you adopted them out? You giving me all access to them doesn't help them then. My rights haven't been established yet, and they need to be."

He hated that she was right. Again. "You're obviously thinking much more clearly than I am at this point," he conceded, not feeling a whole lot better.

And yet…putting those little ones to bed…

That was…something else.

Outside his realm of expectation.

Beyond anywhere he'd tried to reach.

Unforgettable.

In a frighteningly wonderful way.

Dare he tell Mia that he was actually, maybe, toying with the idea of keeping the girls? To the point of looking up preschool options and making a mental list of people he worked with closely, people he trusted who had kids so he could pick their brains if, by some chance, he packed up his charges and took them home with him.

"I don't have nearly as much to consider as you do, Jordon," she pointed out and for a sick second there, he thought she'd read his mind.

In the past, she'd often known what he'd been thinking.

They weren't in the past, and she didn't know him anymore.

"I'm just the babysitter who wants to be a forever visitor," she continued, sounding…healthy.

Maybe too healthy?

Where was the woman who wore her heart on her sleeve? Who bled for a couple she'd never met to the point of wanting to give her own eggs so that another woman could have the child she so desperately wanted?

The woman who'd cried a river the night he'd told her he'd accepted a financial position in New York?

"You're trying to attend to the estate of strangers, while making choices that will affect the entire future lives of two children you just met." She sounded so reasonable. So…calm and sure. Like she had a handle on every aspect of their unexpected reunion.

Her words brought his panic back. Full throttle.

How could he possibly, on his own, with absolutely zero experience with children, handle such a responsibility in a way that those little girls deserved?

Didn't the world see how unfair this was to Brown Eyes and Blue Eyes?

"You're as much a part of them as I am," he said, like a petulant kid.

"I know. And I'm doing all I can."

She was doing more than he was, at the moment. Caring for the girls nonstop while he sat in a luxurious hotel working his regular day job.

"Maybe it would be good if we talked about some of the choices I have to make," he said then. She wanted rights. He could give them to her.

"You probably wouldn't like anything I have to say on the matter."

"As you've pointed out, they're as much your daughters as they are mine. I'm kind of obligated to listen," he said.

"Not legally."

"No, but otherwise…"

"And if I said I thought they should stay here in Shelter Valley?"

She would think that because she'd never lived anywhere else. Hell, she'd hardly spent the night outside of Shelter Valley's ten square mile radius. She'd never been capable of even imagining life outside her remote, small desert town.

But he got her point.

The issues that had broken them apart still existed. In full force. Made larger by the fact that she no longer trusted him.

"They're city girls," he said. And then, against his judgment, added, "When I said choices I have to make, I meant in terms of a Phoenix adoption, or taking them to New York first, which would give me more time to find the best prospective family. And what to keep, maybe put in storage and what to sell of their parents' belongings."

When silence fell, he started to panic again. He needed her. More than that, the girls needed her. Whether she liked it or not.

She didn't have to trust him.

He just needed her to help him.

"Madeline and Keith had a dossier on me," he pointed out to her. "They knew I own an apartment in the city. Pretty clearly, they were choosing to have their daughters raised with all of the opportunities big-city living provides."

Or, it could be, as Kelly Chase had pointed out on Sunday, that the Robinsons' greatest desire was to have their children raised with biological family.

They hadn't known about Mia.

Nor known how much Jordon was going to need help.

She was petitioning for rights. Had already filed the motion. What did he do with that? If he chose to keep the girls, he'd have Mia in his life, too. There, but never his.

If he gave them up, he'd have to find a family willing to take Mia on.

What was she thinking?

The court might not grant her request.

"Please, Mia. At least give me your input in terms of their stuff, and whether to keep them in Phoenix or move them to New York." When it came to those two tiny girls, he'd beg if he had to.

Her continued hesitation gave him serious pause—time to sit face-to-face with the fact that he hadn't included possibly keeping them himself in the choices he'd laid out to her. But when she said, "I'm open to either of those conversations," he took her at face value just enough to say, "Let's start with the boxes, then. Tomorrow night after the girls are asleep."

And when she agreed, he hung up, fully aware that he was in way over his head, but seeing no other option, except to keep pushing forward.

Chapter Nine

When the phone rang while she was still in her office later that night, Mia wanted to push to end the call. She'd spent an hour on her various social media sites, uploading new videos from her queue, responding to comments and posting comments on a couple of accounts she followed. Another half hour took care of financial matters, mostly just going over a report from her accountant. And the rest of the nearly three hours since she'd hung up from Jordon had been spent on reading about Madeline and Keith Robinson. She'd already read and reread all of the files on the girls, the child life specialist's report, even the one from the friend—a next-door neighbor whose daughter was also four—who'd had the twins the previous week but had shied away from the couple's personal business until that evening.

Jordon had mentioned that the couple had read his dossier. That they'd chosen him to be the girls' guardian knowing that his life was in Manhattan. Insinuating that they were choosing big-city life for their daughters' futures.

She'd found supporting evidence to that claim based on their own lifestyle choices. And was in no mood to speak to Jordon again that night. It was almost midnight.

On the third ring—a vibration only as she'd turned off the ringer so it didn't disturb the girls—she glanced at the caller ID. She'd told Jordon she'd answer every call from him anytime she had Ruby and Violet.

When she saw her oldest sibling's name on the screen—her brother, Lincoln—she grabbed up the cell. "What's wrong?"

"That's what I want to know. Have you lost your mind, Mia?"

"Excuse me?"

"It took you years to get over that man. Sara says you still aren't there, which is why you're alone and not starting a family of your own. And you're suddenly watching his kids for him?"

The joys of living in Shelter Valley far outshone the downside. But it did have one. She should have figured someone would call Sara or Lincoln. Both still had friends in the valley. People they'd graduated high school with, who, like Mia, had opted to stay in town.

"Their...parents...just died in an accident, Lincoln. They were referred to Forever Friends. You want me to just turn them away because Jordon Lawrence was appointed their guardian?" She cringed as she heard first, the lie by omission, and then second, her weak defense. She almost had sent them to another program. Right up until she'd found out they were her own children.

Not something anyone but Jordon and now her attorney and several people at Sierra's Web even knew about. If any of them, other than Jordon, shared her news, they'd be liable to a lawsuit. Whether anyone outside Sierra's Web knew about Jordon's biological connection to Ruby and Violet, she had no idea. He hadn't said. She hadn't asked.

But she knew she wasn't going to be the one to spread that truth around.

"And Sara's wrong," she added. She loved her gynecologist sister to death but hated how Sara thought she knew Mia better than Mia knew herself just because Sara was four years older than she was. "I love my life. And I'm far from alone. I can't remember the last time I went twenty-four hours without seeing and talking to multiple people."

"You're keeping Jordon's kids, Mia. What are you thinking?"

Lincoln loved her. She adored him, too, most of

the time. But he was not, as he seemed to think, a replacement for their father.

"I'm thinking that Jordon is in over his head. The kids were here in Phoenix, and he hasn't been back here since he hightailed it out after graduation."

"He was back six years ago to move his mother east with him."

"The girls are only four. They're traumatized. And Jordon is floored. He'd never even met them. He's got all kinds of things to sort out, and with no warning that this all was coming. He's had to work some, too, and he didn't know anyone else to ask."

"So once again, you step up for him. You have his back. When has he ever had yours?"

Ten years ago, before graduation, she'd have had a list of times come to mind. Current day, looking back, she couldn't think of any.

Didn't mean they weren't there.

"He used you, Mia. You don't owe him anything…"

"Believe me," her voice filled with confidence, "I know that. I'm not doing it for him."

"Please tell me you aren't falling for his kids."

Not Jordon's kids, no. "I'm not."

She was falling for her own. But until she knew if she'd have any rights to them, that news was entirely under wraps. Spreading it around served no purpose for anyone.

Including Ruby and Violet.

Most of all them. Not that they'd get the nuances at four. But later…

They'd already lost one mother. She wasn't going to be responsible for them knowing they'd lost another.

"How long are they going to be there?"

"Not long. Maybe another week." If she was lucky enough. "Mariah Macy's Mom is working with them." She paused as she heard herself repeat the girls' name for the horse therapist. And then quickly explained to her brother, who'd known Mariah Montford as long as she had.

"What about Lawrence? He hanging around, too?"

"No. I'm not a fool, you know? He's been here a few hours the past couple of nights, but I leave him alone with the girls." For the most part. They'd had dinner together once. Sort of. She'd served the girls and stood at the counter as much as she could, leaving Jordon to fend for himself.

And then, far too late in the conversation for her liking, she got her game back. "Who's your watchdog?" she asked, going on the defensive, as she should have from the beginning.

But she knew. Greg Richards. Sheriff of Shelter Valley Greg Richards. Greg and Lincoln had become forever friends, in spite of Greg being ten years older, the year Lincoln had risked his life to rescue Greg's adopted son, Ryan, from a raccoon attack.

"You can't honestly think, in Shelter Valley, that someone wouldn't have said something? All the people you have coming and going out there..."

He wasn't going to tell her.

Which was probably just as well. She didn't want to have to be openly pissed at Greg, whom she adored, for caring about her. Even if he went about it in an unbecoming way.

"Seriously, be careful, sis."

"Always."

With a quick "love you," he hung up.

It wasn't until a good minute later that she realized she hadn't asked about his kids. Something she always did. Every single time they talked.

So maybe there'd been a little bit of truth in Lincoln's worries about her. She'd been warned. And would do better guarding her heart, so that when Jordon Lawrence left town this time—possibly taking her little girls with him—she wouldn't face-plant again.

On Wednesday, Jordon spent more time on the business of being Ruby and Violet's guardian. Madeline and Keith had named a close friend of theirs to handle their funeral arrangements, which had all happened before Jordon was in town. He had the estate because they'd left everything material to their twins. After the final bell rang in New York—and going with the thought that since the twins hadn't asked about their house, it would be best just to keep moving them on from it—he interviewed and hired a company to go through the home and get him a full list of items, down to how many spoons in the silverware drawer.

He wanted it all. From laundry detergent to toothpaste. Maybe he'd pass on brand information so the twins had what familiarity they could as they started new lives.

Once he had a list, he'd have something concrete from which to start making decisions. He'd like Mia's opinion, too.

Probably.

She didn't trust him.

And maybe they were more enemies than partners in this life-changing venture. She wasn't going to want what he wanted and vice versa. They'd already been around that block and neither had fared well.

They couldn't chance the same outcome for the girls.

And how would it be any different? She wanted them to stay in Shelter Valley?

She hadn't actually said so, but her question, while hypothetical, had very clearly been asked to prove a point.

Still, no matter what the court said, Mia was their mother. He had to at least listen to her opinions. It was the right thing to do.

This time around, he'd really listen, not just hear what he thought would ultimately happen.

Or assume he knew what was best for her.

But the girls…he had to do what he thought was

best for them. They were too young to know. Or to be expected to make such decisions.

The weight of that…knowing that his choices were going to entirely shape two young lives…he couldn't seem to get out of the mud on that one.

He arrived in Shelter Valley later than he'd have liked. Missed dinner. But brought ice-cream bars. Ruby and Violet had never had them, not with white ice cream on a stick with chocolate covering them, they'd said. While Mia handled some business in her office, he'd taken the twins outside to eat the potentially messy treat just before bath time.

Feeling pleased with himself as the girls grinned and ate like perfectly well-adjusted preschoolers—not the quieter version of themselves they generally were around him—he grabbed his phone out for a picture.

Got two before the world fell apart again.

Ruby took a disastrous bite that broke her melting chocolate and it fell to the ground in a huge chunk.

The little girl started to cry as though her heart was irrevocably broken. Sobs, hiccups, high squeals.

Violet watched her, continuing to eat.

And Jordon felt like everyone on the ranch—however many bunches of acres it was—was hearing the little girl's despair and judging him.

He was a poor excuse for a father.

Even for a guardian.

Kneeling down, as Ruby bent to pick up the dust-covered chocolate, Jordon further upset her by pulling her hand away. He'd been gentle, barely touching her, but she screamed like he'd broken her all over again.

"Hey," he said, trying to get her to look at him, her eyes so filled with tears he wasn't sure sight was even a possibility. "We've got more inside," he told her. "This is why we came outside. The chocolate breaks sometimes."

Why hadn't he bought the fruit juice frozen on a stick kind? The worst they did was drip. Not fall apart in huge heart-destroying clumps.

"Yeah, see, Wuby?" Violet suddenly spoke, didn't seem any louder than Jordon had, but Ruby suddenly stopped crying. "Mine just did it, too!" She pointed to a glob of chocolate on the ground. "Can I have another one, too?"

Not sure if he'd started a bad thing, offering seconds, Jordon sure as hell wasn't going to go back on what he'd said, and had the girls follow him to the steps outside the back door, ordering them not to move any of their feet even a little or they wouldn't get another bar, as he quickly ducked inside for a visit to the freezer.

And came face-to-face with Mia, who'd been watching them from the kitchen doorway.

She handed him two ice-cream bars without a word and headed back in the direction of her office.

What she thought of him, of the whole situation, he had no idea.

And he wasn't going to ask.

* * *

"They didn't finish them."

Mia had just entered the spare bedroom with the boxes, having been summoned by a text from Jordon, and stood in her denim shorts, red tank and flip-flops, feeling like a ranch hand, rather than a successful owner as she faced Jordon in his dark dress pants and white shirt. Even with dust on his shoes, they looked expensive. "I don't care if they did," she said, more in answer to his defensive tone than to the words themselves.

"I didn't want you to think I'd resort to letting them make themselves sick just to get over a tantrum."

"I wouldn't have handed them to you if I thought they'd get sick off them," she pointed out. With as much of the treat as had been falling on the ground and getting all over the twins' hands, faces and clothes, she didn't figure they each got one whole bar inside of them.

She didn't tell him that, though. Didn't want him to know she'd come back out of the office to watch the second go-round, too.

She'd missed all of their first experiences growing from baby to toddler. And would likely miss most of their future ones, as well.

But at least she had first ice-cream bars. Via voyeurism.

"Their dirty clothes hamper is getting full," he said then, referring to the basket she'd pointed out to him the first night he'd taken over bath time. "I'll take it with me in the morning and drop it off at the hotel laundry."

Almost ready to nod, to make certain, with her brother's late night phone call still ringing in her ears, that she wasn't letting Jordon use her, Mia shook her head, instead. "Don't be ridiculous. I'll throw them in with mine."

Not for Jordon. Or to make his life easier.

But because she might not have other opportunities to do her daughters' laundry. If hoarding the memories she was making turned out to be a bad thing for her emotionally, she'd deal with the fallout.

To her way of thinking, those memories were going to be the only comfort she'd have in the years ahead if the court chose not to let her see the twins again once Jordon took them away. Because no matter what the law said, no matter what rights were given to whom, she was a mother who had two little girls who owned her heart whether they ever knew it or not.

It wasn't a law thing. Or even an earthly thing.

Those babies had come from her body.

Nothing anyone said was going to change that. Now that she'd met Ruby and Violet, nothing was going to sever the bond she felt to them.

Love was greater than people.

And choices.

Even her own.

Chapter Ten

It made sense for Mia to do the girls' laundry. So why was it an effort for him to just nod and accept her offer?

He wanted to take the dirty clothes back and have the hotel laundry do it for him. He had to do his own, anyway, too.

But it made sense that the clothes stay where the girls were. And he didn't want to rock Mia's boat.

Not sure what was going on with him, Jordon brushed aside his uneasiness and pulled picture frames out of the box he'd opened.

"I think we should casually introduce one of these to wherever the girls sleep, you know, just put it on the dresser or nightstand without making a big deal of it. And make it a constant for them, wherever they sleep, at least while they transition," Mia said, taking a picture of Keith and Madeline sitting on a rock by the ocean, with Ruby and Violet on a smaller rock right in front of them. "This is a good one because it's away from home. On vacation. Time out of time."

She'd read Mariah O'Connell's report, too. He'd known that. And liked how she'd taken it in enough to be quoting the child life specialist's words almost verbatim. References to Keith and Madeline would serve the girls better if they could be done in time out of time. Keep the people alive, not the life the girls would never be able to go back to.

He took the photo she handed back to him, set it aside. "Good call. Thank you." Relief flooded him. He was busy considering the huge decisions pressing on him and had forgotten that part of Mariah O'Connell's report until she mentioned it.

Which was why he needed Mia.

He focused on details, numbers, with an eye always on the future. Mia lived life with her heart. Making the most out of every moment she was in.

Why hadn't he seen that difference in them before?

Glancing up, his chest tight, Jordon was ready to apologize once more, for not seeing more clearly who she'd been, when the words clogged in his throat.

The picture in her hand was one he'd just handed her. A framed eight-by-ten of Madeline and Keith in the hospital, right after the girls were born. They were sitting together on the hospital bed, each holding a baby with a little pink cap.

Madeline, whose face was sweaty, hair askew and had an IV line hooked up to her arm, had clearly just given birth.

Mia just kept staring, looking like she might cry, her eyes slightly glassy and her lips trembling. Because she hadn't been the one to birth her own babies? Because she never got the ones she'd thought she'd have when the time was right? Because a happy couple was gone, just four short years after that picture had been taken?

Because two little girls were orphans?

Seeming to come back to the present, Mia glanced up with a jerk, her expression smoothing out to bland, as she set the photo in the pack away in storage to give to the girls when they were older pile. "She'd just gone through what I hear is the worst pain ever, twice, and her smile. She looked so happy…"

So she was feeling for the new mother who'd struggled for so long to have children and only got four short years?

Or was her grief more personal?

In the past he hadn't even have had the wherewithal to wonder. Anytime she'd been emotional, his job had been to lighten her moment.

Or so he'd thought.

"You didn't get the children you'd planned to have by the time you were thirty." Regret ripped through him. Not because of his choice to leave; he'd do it again, every time. But because that choice had hurt her so badly.

"Nope."

He regretted that, too. Along with the fact that he'd been too…unaware…to see what he'd been doing to her. To realize that the woman he wanted her to be, the woman he saw her as, hadn't been who Mia Jones was.

Was he doing it again? Bringing the girls to her… he'd been thinking of them. Of himself, yes, but because of his fear that he'd make mistakes with them.

But what about Mia?

"I shouldn't have brought them to you." He'd had no right to rip open her heart again.

Her glance was instant that time, too. But was sharp. Certain. And lingered. "Oh, yes, you should have, Jordon. I deserved to know they'd been orphaned, just like you did."

He'd thought so, too.

And then her gaze softened on his. For a second there, he was twenty-one again, happy to be with the woman he was certain he would spend the rest of his life with. "Even if I never see them again after this week…I will cherish these days forever," she told him.

And he knew, if he did end up keeping the girls— something he wasn't ready to discuss with himself yet—but if he did end up keeping them, Mia would always have the right to see them. To be in contact with them. No matter what the court decided.

"All these years, I've pictured you with a husband and the houseful of kids you wanted."

"I only wanted two."

To him, living in an apartment in New York, two was a houseful.

And he had to know…

"You been in any serious relationships over the years?" Please let it be so. If he'd hurt her so badly that he'd turned her off love…

"Yeah."

Relief came again, a sweet headiness that left as quickly as it came. Turned out, he didn't like knowing that some other man had held his place in Mia's life.

He was really losing it.

He didn't want the woman she was, but he didn't want anyone else to have her? He'd been ignorant, hadn't seen what was right in front of him, but he wasn't a selfish jerk.

He also never wasted time wanting what he couldn't have.

"I haven't," he told her, needed her to know that. "After hurting you, I've made certain that any woman I'm with knows that my career, being in Manhattan, comes first."

Complete truth.

That hit him upside the head. How could he even think about keeping Brown Eyes and Blue Eyes, bringing them into his home, unless he could put them first?

Was he doing to those girls what he'd done to Mia? Building some imaginary picture in his head, thinking he could have people like he had things?

Without considering that people had needs and things didn't?

Going cold, feeling himself pale, Jordon glanced at the picture he held, a younger version of Ruby and Violet, and felt a deep pang. He wasn't going to let them down.

Mia, in shorts that left too much of her long, tanned legs showing and a tank top that reminded him of how those breasts felt in his hands, was watching him.

Seeing too much?

"Who?" he blurted, an immediate diversion from himself. "What happened?" And then, at her startled expression, added, "Your serious relationship. Were you married?"

Had the guy died? Was her grief more than he'd even considered?

Was he just screwing up everywhere?

That was why he stuck with the numbers. The trades. The place where he could channel his adrenaline overload and count on himself to get it right most of the time.

"I was engaged."

Jordon had asked her to marry him their sophomore year. She'd said yes on the spot and had thrown herself across his body, kissing him with a passion he'd never known since her.

"To an economist," she added, drawing a picture he was pretty sure he didn't want to see. An economist. A man who studied the distribution of wealth. Who studied finance.

A man who'd need to be in the thick of things.

Just like Jordon.

"I met him through Lincoln," she said. "He was in Phoenix, studying the rapid growth of the city, which is now the fifth biggest city in the United States," she said. "He worked for a national development company. Had studied New York's and Los Angeles's growth patterns, was helping them determine where and how to build communities to fit the area…"

Was she trying to show him she could do as well or better than him? He'd never, for one second, doubted that.

"What happened?" he asked but didn't really want to hear the ending to the story. He knew it already. Had lived it.

"I changed my mind."

"Because he wanted you to leave Shelter Valley?"

"To the contrary," Mia said, pulling a photo album out of the box they were taking far too long to get through. "He's still here. He loves Shelter Valley. He has his doctorate degree. Had written some pretty impressive papers on macroeconomics, and when I introduced him to Will Parsons—who's still president of Montford University by the way—Will knew who he was. Offered him a job. My ex is now head of the economics department. We're still good friends."

Well, wasn't that something. The man was right there, a professor at their alma mater.

And Mia was good friends with him.

But hadn't married him.

Because Jordon had blown her ability to trust a man that much. Any man? Or just men from the city who tracked money movement for a living?

She didn't say so.

He didn't ask.

But he got her message.

Loud and clear.

Mia was glad when Jordon called a sudden halt to the unboxing after that first box. She needed him gone.

"It's a lot coming at us at once," she said as she followed him to the door. Trying to make something better that never would be.

"It's my problem, Mia. You need to do what's best for you."

Sounded…odd…coming from him. The guy who'd been so certain he knew what was best for everyone. Who, instead of listening to her, or trying to understand, had just kept telling her to trust him. She'd love New York, she'd see. He'd been so jazzed about his perfect job offer, too excited to sleep even, the first night after the opportunity had arrived. Just kept saying he knew her and he knew she'd love it.

Truth was, he hadn't known her.

"I am doing what's best for me, Jordon," she said then.

He studied her for a long moment but didn't say anything else. Not even good-night. He just quietly let himself out.

Mia checked on the girls and stood there over-flowing as she watched their little bodies, cuddled up together, expand and contract with breathing, almost as one. Pulling her phone out of her pocket she took more than a dozen pictures, none of which were going to turn out well because she'd turned off her flash so she didn't wake them.

And then, baby monitor in hand, she poured herself a glass of wine. Set both down on a shelf in her bathroom, made for that purpose. Ran a bubble bath in her garden tub, stripped down and climbed in, crying as she splashed water on her face.

As though she could hide the tears she could no longer hold back.

Looking at the picture of Madeline Robinson with the babies she'd just birthed, the look on the other woman's face...the ethereal joy, excitement and peace mixed perfectly—that was motherhood.

Madeline was Ruby and Violet's mother.

Not Mia.

What an ironic twist of fate, that the woman who'd fought to have them, who'd agonized birthing them, got such little time with them. And Mia, who'd barely given those eggs a thought once she'd donated them, might get to be in their lives for the next fourteen years.

Didn't seem right.

Or fair.

And maybe...just maybe...she cried for the young woman inside her who still loved Jordon Lawrence. She didn't trust him. Didn't want him in her life.

But standing there watching him with the girls and their ice cream that evening...she'd remembered so many other times he'd stepped in to help someone who was struggling, coming up with solutions.

She'd playfully called him the fix-it man. Always thinking he had to solve everyone else's problems. Always certain that he *could* solve them.

And going the extra mile to do so.

He'd gotten it right with the twins. They'd wanted more ice cream.

With Mia...he'd been unable to give her the solution she'd needed. But, while he hadn't known her nearly as well as he'd thought he had, as she'd thought he had—maybe she hadn't known him well enough, either.

Because she honestly hadn't known that he couldn't be happy making his money transactions from Phoenix, or over the internet at home in Shelter Valley. There were banks everywhere. And not all successful money men were physically on Wall Street doing what they did.

She'd told him from the beginning, before she'd

gone out with him, that she wasn't ever going to leave
Shelter Valley, and he'd said okay.

And then he'd kissed her.

And…

It had happened that way every time she'd mentioned her future in Shelter Valley. Even the night
he'd asked her to marry him. She'd said yes, as long
as he was happy staying in Shelter Valley.

He'd said okay. And then he'd kissed her.

And…she'd thrown her body on top of his and
given him every single thing she had to give.

Reaching for her wine, Mia took a gulp. Trying
to swallow back her sobs.

She wasn't successful.

Chapter Eleven

The girls had been in his custody for four nights and he hadn't slept even once under the same roof with them.

Nor had he made any decisions regarding their future.

While he wallowed in some kind of self-imposed la-la land, the twins were settling into a new sense of normal.

One that wouldn't be permanent.

Meaning he'd have to upend their worlds again.

Nothing he could do about some of that. Adoptions took time. It could be a while before they were in their forever homes.

And Mariah O'Connell and Kelly had both said that children adapt.

Still, as he sat at the desk in his suite before dawn Thursday morning, already signed in to be present electronically when the first bell rang, he made a decision.

He had to share a roof with the girls.

Without shipping them back to sad-waif zone.

He had to know them well enough to know what decisions would be best for them.

As a plan, there were obvious holes. But at least he'd made a choice on their behalf. Looking around the suite, he imagined a delivery of a roomful of toys and books and gadgets appropriate to four-year-olds.

Bringing them back to the city would probably be good for them. They were city girls. Were used to riding in car seats with traffic and colorful sights whizzing by them. Sensitizing their imaginations.

Planting seeds that would grow into ideas for future opportunities, needs, wants.

From what he'd been told, prior to their parents' deaths, Ruby and Violet had been social little girls seemingly afraid of very little. They'd been adventurous. Willing, eager even, to try new things. And would carry on conversations with adults as though they were capable of holding their own. As long as their parents, or people they knew and trusted, were around.

He had to preserve those outgoing little personalities. Not let his own lack of clarity lock them in a world that they'd be afraid to leave.

The bell rang, calling him, before he got as far as

making any online purchases. And by the time he'd finished for the day, he was rethinking the filling the room with toys portion of his plan. The girls already had two rooms worth of toys. In boxes at Mia's place.

And he'd already asked Ruby and Violet's biological mother to go through their things with him. To see what they owned. What they liked. What they might need immediately, and what might be better packed away for a while.

The little ballet shoes were definitely a wait item. At least until they were back in New York. No point in getting the girls all worked up and wanting to dance without an avenue planned for them to do so.

He could still bring the boxes to his suite.

Would Mia be willing to take a couple of days of vacation and stay at the hotel? Maybe watch the girls during the day so he didn't have to transition them to a stranger babysitter while he worked? He could get her a suite on the same floor.

All expenses paid by him, of course.

She could take the girls to the resort's huge outdoor pool. And maybe to the children's museum Mariah O'Connell had talked about. Assuming they hadn't just recently been there with their parents...

As much as she loathed leaving Shelter Valley, he was pretty certain she'd comply. For the girls.

Decision made, Jordon booked the suite. Figured it was meant to be when he was able to get one just two doors down from his. The girls could spend time

in both suites, though Mia's only had the one bedroom so they'd be staying with him.

He was on a roll. Finally getting things done.

And set off for Shelter Valley with a smile on his
face.

Mia was lying in a chaise watching the activities
in the shallow end of the pool when her phone rang.
Jordon.

It wasn't even four yet. He had to be calling to let
her know he'd be late. Or maybe not make it at all
that night.

Part of her hoping it was the latter, she answered,
"Hello?"

"I'm letting you know I'm pulling in," he said.

She sat up straight. "Here?"

When a couple of the guest parents and the instructor in the pool looked over at her, she sat back,
and more quietly asked, "You're at the ranch?"

"Yeah." No explanation. Which told her more was
coming.

Dread filled her. Had he found someone who
wanted to adopt the girls? Was he going to take
them?

She thought about the cabin she'd reserved for
him.

And hadn't yet told him about.

Because she wasn't sure she trusted herself to have
him around that much.

"We…um…aren't up there," she said, watching as

first Ruby and then Violet, both wearing their new water wing vests, put their faces in the water and pulled them back up laughing.

She'd missed the picture. And blamed Jordon.

A shameful second.

She'd had a few of them where he was concerned. And after her cry the night before, was over herself.

"We're at the pool," she said, looking around for her wrap. "The girls met a couple of kids staying in the cabins," she said. "When they were with Macy this morning," she quickly added, realizing she should never have taken the twins to the pool without letting Jordon know. "They had so much fun, I thought… I brought them to swim lessons," she admitted.

"Swim lessons?" His tone didn't bode so horribly. He sounded more perplexed than anything.

"It's all part of the dude ranch," she told him. "Afternoon swim lessons for anyone eight or younger who wants them. It's just beginning stuff, and we sell water wings at the pool and the girls are both securely strapped into theirs."

"What pool?"

"It's down by the cabins."

"You have a pool?"

"Yeah."

"You didn't mention it."

Hadn't seemed pertinent. Not like swimming lessons were.

"I'm sorry I didn't text, Jordon. I should have

made sure you were okay with them being in the pool."

"I didn't know you had a pool." He seemed lost in that particular piece of minutia.

"With swim lessons," she added inanely.

"Down by the cabins."

Had he been drinking? She'd never known Jordon to over-imbibe. To the contrary, he'd always been designated driver when he'd gone out with friends.

"Yeah," she said, pulling a towel up to her chest in lieu of the wrap she couldn't immediately locate.

"I'm on my way down now."

"Um…we can meet you up there," she blurted, standing. "I'll get the girls out of the pool and…"

"I'm already here."

Her gaze met his across the length of the water as he hung up and let himself inside the gated pool enclosure.

She could feel his look as though he was touching her, though he was the one gaining attention from everyone else—mostly mothers of little ones—in the area. He was the only one fully dressed. The only one on the entire ranch in business clothes.

And he was gorgeous.

She, on the other hand, was not dressed. Wrapping her towel around her waist, pushing a hand through her always-messy short blond hair, she straightened her shoulders and took pride in her tightly muscled feminine form.

He'd seen it all before.

Ten years hadn't changed much.

As he drew closer, and her nipples tightened with desire, she dragged her mind out of the gutter—out of her past—and focused fully back on the two four-year-old blondes listening to the eighteen-year-old teacher in the pool.

And then, on the count of three, drawing in breath and putting their faces in the water again.

"They're not afraid of the water." Jordon's voice beside her sent electrical shivers through Mia. She needed to step away from him.

Didn't know how to do so without being obvious. He couldn't know she was still attracted to him. She couldn't give him that edge.

Or mess up things that could come back on the girls.

"They're like two little commodores," she said. "Whether it's climbing up a ladder and sliding onto a horse's back or jumping into a pool, they're game to give it a try." If he heard the pride in her voice, he didn't call her on it.

She couldn't take back the words.

Wasn't even sure she wanted to.

Those two little warriors were not her legal children, but they were each half of her. Whatever genes carried grit, determination…and blond hair. And Violet had her eyes.

"I'm sorry I didn't let you know I was bringing them down here." Truth was, she hadn't even thought about letting Jordon know. She had been focused on blocking out all thoughts of Jordon since her break-down in the tub the night before.

"I need to have them spend the night under the same roof as me."

The statement was bald.

And wasn't a suggestion.

"I have a cabin available for you starting Saturday," she blurted. Out there by the pool, underneath the blinding and beautiful hot Arizona sun, she felt safer. As though nothing could hurt as badly as she'd thought she'd been hurting the night before.

"A cabin." He looked over at her and she made herself hold that gaze. And nod.

Then said, "I figured you'd want to stay with them."

With a cock of his head, he studied her, looked as though he was weighing words, and then Ruby squealed, and they both looked instantly back at the water.

"I did it!" Ruby's voice carried to them. "I swimmed!"

She was standing two or three feet from where she'd been. And when those vivid blue eyes turned toward Mia, she was grinning, and clapping, feeling as though her heart might burst.

Until Ruby turned back to the instructor, and Mia's gaze collided with Jordon's.

"Until you know where they're going, I figured you'd want them to stay in therapy with Macy," she said. "I added the swim lessons as a whim, mostly because they seemed to have fun with the other little kids this morning. I explained that the kids are only here for the week, and then new kids would be coming. I thought it might help them to adjust to having new people come and go from their lives, while Macy was a constant. Anyway…it's all up to you, of course."

And that was the bottom line. The decision was rightfully Jordon's.

And until the court gave her some rights, *if* the court acknowledged her maternity at all, she had to acquiesce to whatever Jordon thought was best.

He glanced out to the pool, watching as Violet took her turn "swimming" and then glanced over at them, grinning, as she came up for air. "Did you see that, Mama Mia?" she called.

Mia nodded, immediately cringing over the fact that Jordon wasn't also acknowledged, and unable to stop the huge smile that spread across her face, or the tears that swam in her eyes for a second as she called out, "Good job!" to Violet.

"Good job!" Jordon called out as an echo, but Violet had already turned back to her instructor.

"It's just because I'm with them all day, from the time they get up," she said then. "If you stay at the cabin, and you're the one getting them up and feeding them in the morning, all the routine stuff of living, they'll look to you, too."

"I'm not bothered that they're turning to you, Mia," he said, his tone almost gentle. "I just need to know them better. I need to see them in their own environment. It's the only way I can make decisions that are in their best interests."

"Okay."

But it wasn't. Not for her.

She knew it before he said, "I'm planning to take them with me back to the city."

"When?"

"Tomorrow. That'll give me two full days to get acclimated with them before I have to work again."

And knew, too, that when the words came, all she could do was nod.

Because she had no rights.

"Daddy's goned with Mommy and he's not coming back." Brown Eyes, expression wide and solemn, said as Jordon, sitting at the end of the queen-size bed in Mia's house, turned the page on a book about animals saying good-night.

Did he nod and keep reading?

Seemed like the chicken's way out. And kind of heartless, too.

"I know, sweetie." And he thought of what Mariah O'Connell, the child life specialist, had said. "But you know how you got a happy feeling, and seemed all warm inside when he hugged you?"

Both girls nodded.

"That doesn't ever go away. It's called love and Mommy and Daddy will always love you."

"I think Mama Mia loves us," Ruby said then.

And Violet shook her head. "She hasn't seen us be bad, yet. Mommy said when you love someone you love them even when they're bad. 'Member?" Such wisdom coming from a tiny voice with *w* sounds where there should be *r*'s.

Ruby's nod was exaggerated, her blue eyes wide. "We got water on the floor! That was bad."

"And we spilled our chocolate on the ground," Violet said slowly, turning her gaze from her sister to stare straight at Jordon. "Do you think that means she could love us?"

Emotion strangling him, Jordon had no words. No wisdom. No answers.

And, in the next moment, when he could breathe, he said, "I'm sure it does."

Might be the wrong thing. To let those children know that they were loved by someone else from whom they were going to be taken away.

But the alternative? To tell them that they weren't loved? Most particularly when he knew for certain that they were?

And if he kept the girls, Mia wouldn't be gone from their lives. She'd be a part of them forever.

And the ranch...the twins could come for summers...kids went to camp...

And he wouldn't need to worry about a full-time nanny. They'd be in school during the year when they were with him, and summering with Mia...

And, and, and...

Was he really thinking about keeping them?

His mind went blank—just as it had when he'd seen way too much of Mia in that sleek black suit, earlier.

And try as he might, Jordon just couldn't get past the blind spots inside of him to find his answers.

Chapter Twelve

As soon as the girls had exited the pool, while they were still wrapped, dripping in their towels, Jordon had announced that he was taking them out to dinner.

He'd invited Mia to go.

Still reeling from his announcement—he was moving the girls to his suite in the city the very next day—she'd declined.

Had eaten leftover vegetable soup and crackers at her desk with her social media family. Seeking the distance she'd known she needed.

Jordon was completely within his rights to take the girls. For all she knew, it was best that he do so. She had no valid case to be angry with him.

But she was.

And as she heard him enter the house with the girls just in time for baths and bed, she knew why.

It wasn't because he was taking the girls. That part had been inevitable. It was because he was taking her heart with him. Again.

Taking the children she'd fallen head over heels in love with.

The past was repeating itself.

And there was nothing she could do about it.

Except…do what she did. Live her life.

He'd broken her ten years before.

But she wasn't a kid anymore. She knew how to cope.

And had Jordon to thank for that.

Still, knowing and feeling were different things.

She'd heard from her lawyer that morning. Her request for visitation had been filed with the court. Jordon would be served notice and have twenty-five days to respond before any further steps would be taken.

Jordon. Jordon. Jordon.

So much rested on Jordon.

When she'd promised herself that she'd never open her heart up to him again.

Staring at her blinking cursor, waiting to hear the front door close behind him so she could breathe freely again—and maybe go peek in on the girls—Mia jumped when her phone binged a text.

You have a minute?

Jordon.

Wanting more of her.

Her first instinct, to ignore him, gave way to the second. Tell him no.

She waited for the third.

Of course, she texted back. And then, not wanting to be closed in her house with him, added, On the porch?

She'd changed back into her shorts and tank top as soon as she'd returned from the pool and in spite of the still-one-hundred-degree heat outside, wanted to pull on a sweater.

Maybe even a coat.

Except she'd have to remember which spare closet she'd stored it in when she'd returned from a family ski trip up north four years before.

Jordon was already seated in one of the wooden rockers on her porch. Looking all successful and confident and way too good in his business pants, shirt and shoes.

And too…comfortable…on the porch that had once hosted him regularly. Even the baby monitor sitting upright on the arm of the love seat beside him seemed to fit right in to the cozy picture.

He'd asked for a minute. Looked like he was planning to stay much longer than that.

As though reading her mind, he leaned forward as soon as she approached. Both feet flat on the ground, his elbows on his knees, he said, "I wanted to speak with you about moving the girls."

Nope. "No need." She had to cut him off at the quick. Didn't trust herself to be fair to him. Stood there, arms crossed as though she was cold, facing him.

"Could you have a seat?"

She could if she wanted to. She didn't want to.

But after a few seconds, thinking only of Ruby and Violet, she sat. She was a mother now. What she felt absolutely did not come first.

Oddly, she didn't even want it to. Putting the girls first felt natural. It was something she didn't just need to do. She wanted to do it.

Steepling his fingers, Jordon looked at them long enough that Mia felt a twinge of compassion for him. The man hadn't asked for any of what was happening to them. But he'd stepped up completely. Taking on an overwhelming responsibility with the same focus and effort he'd once given to her.

Jordon had always given one thousand percent. He'd always tried.

He just hadn't listened…

Glancing up at her, he opened his mouth. Closed it again. Took a breath. "I…rented a suite for you, too."

She heard him. Could repeat the words. Couldn't understand them.

"Before you go off on me, hear me out," he said while she was still staring, open-mouthed, frozen in place.

Elation warring with dread.

He was doing it again. Thinking if he could just

get her to leave Shelter Valley everything would work out fine.

Ten years ago, it had been for him. For them.

And now...for their daughters?

She was going. No question about that. For Violet and Ruby, she'd move to the moon in a clown suit.

Even knowing that it was only temporary. That when he found a permanent family for the girls, she could possibly never see them again.

Or she could.

Either way, she was in, completely.

"I didn't factor in the daily horse therapy."

What was that?

His frown seemed more a sign of being perplexed than displeased.

He had her full attention.

"They're city girls," he said then. "I think it's good for them to have some reality in their lives so that they don't just adjust to a vacation-type life."

He thought her life a vacation? She worked damned hard...

It wasn't about her. And he didn't look like he had any idea he'd just slammed her.

Because he hadn't been talking about her life on the ranch.

He was reaching out to her, sincerely, for the girls' sakes.

Reeling herself in, Mia took a deep breath. Hated that she was so out of character around him. She wasn't an emotionally overwrought person.

To the contrary, she'd always been the one to take things in stride.

Even after he'd left. Once she'd recovered from the initial shock. Figured out how to live with the heartache.

"At the same time, the change in them, in just four days… I talked to Kelly Chase this afternoon, on my way out of Phoenix, and she seemed almost shocked that the girls are sleeping so well, eating so well and seeing them in the pool today…they were laughing. Engaging."

"Like you said, it's vacation time."

With a sideways tilt to his head, he said, "Maybe." But he didn't look convinced.

"I'm thinking…maybe we should take them to the city over the weekend but keep their things here for at least another week."

While she tried to breathe through the constriction in her chest, he continued, "I could move some of my stuff here Saturday morning, into the cabin, and then we could all four go to the city and stay in the suites Saturday night. Come back here Sunday night. I'll keep my suite and use it for work every day. I've already got everything set up there. The connections are top speed and uninterrupted…"

He seemed to be making things up as he went along.

Or figuring them out.

And tears filled her eyes. When Jordon was on, he was really, really good.

She wanted to tell him she didn't have to go, since it was just the one night and he didn't need a babysitter since he wouldn't be working, but she wasn't that big of a person. Because she wanted to soak up every single second with her daughters that she could.

And it wasn't like Jordon was any more permanent in their lives than she was.

Maybe going back and forth between the two of them would prevent the girls from being too attached.

Being with Mia predominantly during the day, but with Jordon at night.

"I'll pay for my own room." Her voice, when she was able to use it, came out soft. Almost a whisper. She wanted to thank him.

Tell him he was doing a great job.

That she was proud of him.

But couldn't.

They weren't…anything to each other anymore.

They were things only to the girls they'd created in another lifetime.

Their gazes met. He studied her for a long moment. And finally nodded.

When he stood, she stood.

And then, with another quick, silent nod, he was gone.

There were bound to be feelings. Jordon told himself it was only logical that residual emotions he'd once felt for Mia would surface as they faced, together, what was, for him, the most intense week of his life.

He'd guess it was for her, too.

The swimsuit…hell, even dusty shorts and cowboy boots…were bound to remind him of a day when he'd been welcome to reach out and touch. When he knew he'd be touched in all the ways that he liked best.

Just as he knew exactly what, where and how to touch Mia to bring her to a pleasure that lit up her eyes and sometimes came out in cries of ecstasy.

You might move on, but the body, the heart, didn't forget.

Remembering…reliving, reexperiencing emotions…was natural.

And so thinking, as Jordon drove home Thursday night, and awoke Friday morning awash in longing and need far beyond sexual, he put those feelings in the box in which they belonged, and set his mind to focusing on their present circumstances.

The workday saved him. Took all of his focus and used up a ton of adrenaline. He closed the day up higher than he'd hoped.

And then, after clearing it with Mia, drove to Shelter Valley early to spend a couple of hours with the girls before dinner so he could make it back to the local investor function to which he'd been invited during online celebrations that morning.

A gathering that included a couple of clients he'd like to add to his list.

Mia had said that there was an outdoor movie for the dude ranch kids that evening and she'd wanted to take Ruby and Violet, so everything had worked out perfectly.

He gained three new clients, instead of two. And went to bed Friday night full of success all around. Brimming with it.

And lay there thinking about the cow and owl who called good-night to each other every night on the farm. The little dog who ran into everyone's room at night to wish them sweet dreams. The moon who never forgot to say good-night.

He hadn't forgotten, either.

He just hadn't been there.

The pang he felt meant nothing. Just a fallout from the highs he'd been on all day. What came up had to come down. Law of nature.

Even if he was a true father, had a family of his own, he wouldn't be home every single night to wish his kids good-night. Sometimes babysitters did that.

But a true dad would know that he'd have a life-time of good-nights ahead of him.

He fell asleep on the thought.

Chapter Thirteen

The mistake Mia made regarding Saturday afternoon and night in the city was that she hadn't figured on how it would work, exactly. One car. The four of them.

At the Phoenix Children's Museum. There'd been so much to do, but the girls, of course, wanted to stick together, to explore all of the floors, the activities, together. To play together. Which forced her and Jordon together, too. With other couples talking to them outside of child-size exhibits, assuming they were together. Parents.

Most particularly with the girls calling out for Mama Mia to watch this or look at that. Jordon seemed to take it all in stride.

Mia was soaking up every second, opening her heart as wide as it could go, soaking in every nuance.

Which also released the well of pain and regret stored there.

While the girls were scientifically hers and Jordon's, they weren't Mom and Dad. They weren't a family.

But by some cruel twist of fate, she was getting a real-life taste of what could have been.

What she'd thought was going to be.

In the Mexican restaurant where the girls wanted to eat quesadillas, she and Jordon sat side by side in a booth because the girls climbed in first, naturally, together.

The waitress assumed they were a family.

And for a moment, Mia let herself pretend.

But only for a moment.

She knew better than to live in a fantasy. The one she'd unknowingly occupied in the past had almost killed her.

Or rather, almost killed her ability to find happiness.

And still, while regret had her fighting back painful tears, her joy was just as profound. She was a mother, out with her children.

A gift she'd begun to think she'd never experience.

One she'd almost convinced herself she didn't really want. Didn't fit the lifestyle she'd ended up making for herself.

Except, of course, it did. She'd built a life ready for children to grow up in. One where she could be present, and be working, too.

Where her children would always have her around, while being exposed to and taught by others, too. Where adventure and lessons in kindness and service, where knowing diverse peoples and their families, would be an everyday part of life.

And where money worries didn't exist.

She tried her best to tune out Jordon, not to ignore him, or to fail to include him, just to keep him away from her heart. And her deepest thoughts.

He'd caught her eye a couple of times. Shared a smile with her, once. And another time, seemed to be contemplating the state of the world judging by his serious, concerned expression, but she didn't have time to dwell on either of them.

It wasn't like energetic and active four-year-old children left any time for serious adult conversation, so mostly she was successful in her stay away from Jordon quest.

And maybe she'd imagined the times of connection.

Like she had the four years they'd been together in the past? She'd been so certain that she and Jordon knew each other as well as they knew themselves.

When, in truth, they apparently hadn't known each other at all.

Not down deep.

But then, he laughed at something Ruby said and her insides leaped in memory of the sound. And when he was explaining to the twins how motors worked,

they could have been back in college and he was helping someone from one of his classes get a concept.

All in all, the day took everything she had, so that
when the girls were finally staying in bed with the
lights out in their room—after having begged Mama
Mia to stay and tuck them in—she was practically
running for the outer door of Jordon's massive suite.

"Can you stay for a minute?" Jordon's voice
stopped her. It was odd-sounding.

Almost…unsure.

So not Jordon.

"Sure." She turned. It wasn't like she had anywhere to be except inside her own door down the
hall. She had her computer, though. Had planned to
spend time on her social media platforms. To schedule projects, videos and posts for the next month's
worth of paid crafting endorsements.

He'd worn a pair of slip-ons with black shorts and
a white, far-too-good-fitting polo shirt that day and
while the girls and the activities had distracted her
from paying too much attention, his broad shoulders,
the vivid blue in his eyes…those thighs…they were
a little harder to ignore alone in the living space of
his suite.

Leaving her far too aware that there was a dining
room with a massive table for twelve and a closed
bedroom door separating them from their soon-to-
be sleeping chaperones.

He'd led the way to the seating area, then segued

to the wet bar. Poured himself a glass of something amber then offered her a glass of wine.

In the process of shaking her head, Mia heard her voice say, "Please." And wasn't sorry that she'd lost a battle with her better judgment. She wanted the wine.

Wanted to relax and get some good work done yet that evening. Her crafting hours were going to be limited, still, for at least another week, which meant she had to be organized. Have a solid course of action to make the best of the time she had.

When he handed her the glass of wine, he held his glass up, as though to toast. And she almost tapped her glass to his. Almost.

It had been tradition. One of many between them. Anytime they shared anything with alcohol in it they'd always made the same toast. "To us."

She couldn't do it. Sipped. And looked down at her white denim skirt and black sleeveless button-down shirt as though she was only just seeing them for the first time.

"You haven't asked about adoption plans."

His words drew her gaze instantly, sharply, in his direction.

"It's not my right…"

"Cut the crap, Mia."

She stared. Wanted to pretend that she didn't know why he was upset.

But she did.

Jordon had been trying all week to include her in his decision-making. To involve her.

He'd wanted her input.

And she'd needed to stay out of it.

"I can't be sure that any opinion I give will be solely in the girls' best interests." She told him part of the truth. The largest part.

But there was more.

She just couldn't be friends with Jordon Lawrence. No matter how many embryos they'd had turned into children.

She'd given him everything. Her heart. Her soul. Her body. Her trust.

No way she could take them back.

No way he could have any of them again.

No way she could pretend to just be friends.

"You don't think your opinions would be in their best interests? Why is that?" He'd taken a seat on the end of the couch, perpendicular to the chair she'd chosen. Seemed content to sit there all night.

"No, Jordon." She shook her head. "You don't get to pick my brain anymore. Or get into my head."

When he nodded, maintaining eye contact, a shock went through her. "I know," he said. "But you said, in terms of Ruby and Violet, that you'd give your opinion. I asked for it. I gave you the right..."

He had.

"Yes, but the court hasn't yet. And when you adopt them out, any right you gave me will be gone," she said, giving him total honesty. Because the moment deserved that much. "I can't pretend again, Jordon. I can't take on something that isn't really mine, not in terms of making decisions for the future. I love them. I will always love them. It's an incredible thing really... I had no idea..."

She was getting off topic. On the girls, yes, but not on anything he needed to know.

"It really is," he said then, a soft glow in his gaze as it caught hers unaware.

She held on.

Couldn't swallow.

Had to blink to save herself.

"So...have you found a family to adopt them, then?" He'd started the conversation with the mention of adoption plans.

She'd been trying to brace herself ever since.

Would never be ready.

"No."

Her relief palpable, Mia took a sip of wine, trying to act as though she had no skin in the matter either way. The court would give her rights, or it wouldn't. Adoption shouldn't change that overly much, her lawyer had explained the day before. Any family considering adoption would be made aware of the motion she'd already filed as it was currently moving through the courts.

The only wrench in the works would come if the potential adoptive family opposed the motion. They'd have the right to file a response, saying so.

But they'd have to prove good reason in terms of the twins' well-being.

She tried to keep herself contained. To not engage. But had to ask, "Then why get on me for not asking?"

"Because it's the most important decision in our daughters' lives," he said, opening his mouth as if to say more, but she shook her head.

Violently. Would have spilled her wine if she hadn't set it down.

"The biology of those children belongs to both of us, Jordon, but we didn't create babies together. We only made embryos. We didn't birth them. Or raise them. They aren't *our* children."

Sucking in his lips some, as though holding them closed to prevent words from escaping, Jordon nodded.

Looked over at her.

Then said, "I'm thinking about keeping them, Mia."

That's when her entire world imploded.

"You...what...you live in New York, and yeah, the Robinsons knew that and gave them to you, but this whole thing was my idea, and you get to raise them?" Mia's stricken expression made Jordon glad that words were tumbling out of her.

Giving him some clue how to help.

"I'm sorry," she said then. "That's not fair to put that on you. You didn't ask for any of this. It's just... you're serious? You're going to keep them?" She was right back in control. Proving once again that she didn't need his help.

His disappointment was far more intense than the situation demanded.

"I was thinking that I'd have them in New York during the school year, and then they'd come here to spend summers at the ranch," he said, testing the theory out loud.

Against his greatest critic.

Because he couldn't find a way to put it down on his own.

And because he fully trusted Mia to put the girls first.

Mouth open, she was staring at him. "You'd let me have them for the summers? They could grow up being a part of Shelter Valley?"

The way she said it, like her hometown was some kind of black hole to him, hit hard. Harder than it should have?

Had he made her feel ashamed of the small town she'd loved more than him?

And...what was that? The mental question hit him on the tail of his last thought.

Did he really believe it? Had he ten years ago?

Mia had loved Shelter Valley more than she'd loved him.

Had he consciously had the thought when he'd left her?

Or was it just now surfacing?

He'd spent so many years blocking it all out, he couldn't be sure.

"There's no way I'd keep them and not share them

with you, Mia. You have to know that. Somewhere, deep down…"

She stared at him and blinked when her eyes grew moist. Then, she shook her head. "No, Jordon. Don't do that to me. We can talk about the girls, about a future that could include both of us in their lives… but don't…"

When her voice broke off, it took all he had not to pull her into his arms. To promise her that everything would be okay and he'd never hurt her again.

But he couldn't do it.

Because he probably would hurt her. Just as she'd hurt him.

They were too different. Maybe not their personalities, or their life views…but their needs. Shelter Valley, or small-town living at least, brought her peace. And had him climbing the walls. While big cities, the freneticism, kept her on edge. And that was where he thrived.

He loved the East Coast.

She was the Wild West through and through.

"You'd really let me have them all summer?"

Her doubt bothered him. Way more than it should have. "They're yours, too, Mia."

She nodded then. Staring at him, still. Sipped from her wineglass without taking her eyes from him.

As though if she blinked, he'd change into some kind of monster.

And the trouble was, he couldn't blame her.

He understood.

She was the one who'd been honest from the very beginning. Before they'd even become a "them." She'd told him she couldn't leave Shelter Valley. That her future was in that remote, small desert town.

And he'd said okay. Every single time.

Over a four-year span.

Every time.

Seeing it all through her eyes, he'd been lying to her their entire relationship.

No way a woman was ever going to be able to trust a man who'd done that to her.

But he could co-parent with her.

Because they both loved those little girls that much.

"Are you in?" he asked, feeling as though his entire life rested on her response.

Which made no sense. He could keep the girls with or without her.

But they needed her.

And she needed them, too.

"I'm in," she said, then stood up, emptied her glass of wine, crossed the suite to peek in on the girls and let herself out.

Chapter Fourteen

Trembling so hard she could hardly get her key card to swipe, Mia fell into her hotel suite and headed straight for the wet bar. She snagged a bottle of water out of the refrigerator behind the bar, made a beeline for an armchair in a seating arrangement in front of the wall of windows and collapsed.

The wall of city lights glistening in front of her blurred as her eyes filled with tears.

Happy ones.

Relief was palpable. And ecstasy…she didn't know what to do with it. She needed Brilliant, her horse. Her private love. Needed to tell the twelve-year-old animal the newest twist in her Jordon Law-rence saga.

Brilliant had only been two when Mia's father had

used grocery money to buy the rescued mustang after Jordon left.

The mare had heard every single thought Mia had had back then. She'd been through all of the feelings. Brilliant had saved her life.

And now…

She was a mother!

Not officially. Not until the court recognized her as such.

But…the carrot he'd dangled…

Would he really let her keep the girls on the ranch for months each year? Months! She'd be a real mother! And maybe she could fly to New York for their birthday, for Christmas…she'd heard the city was beautiful during the holidays. Had always been curious about the huge tree that was decorated in the center there.

She wouldn't stay at Jordon's, of course, but she'd find a place close by. Something with security.

And she wouldn't stay long. The pushing crowds of strangers. The constant noise.

Oh, who cared! She was really going to be a mother!

She couldn't count on it, of course. Couldn't tell anyone.

Jordon could change his mind in a blink.

About keeping the girls. Or keeping her in their lives.

But sitting there in the dark, she couldn't help but savor the possibility. Ruby and Violet. In her life forever?

Being able to watch them grow? To make certain they knew, every day of their lives, that they were loved and adored?

She could video call every morning before school. Or every night before bed.

Maybe both.

And fly to New York for dance recitals.

Or parent-teacher conferences.

If Jordon agreed.

She was getting way too far ahead of herself. Way too greedy. He'd offered summers and she was taking over parts of every single day.

But only in her dreams. Her secret thoughts that she shared only with herself and Brilliant.

Violet and Ruby...if they showed any interest at all in artistic endeavors—and they had already that week—she had so much she could teach them.

She could introduce a kid's corner to her brand.

Oh, God.

She had biological children.

And she was going to get to mother them?

A dream she'd been slowly giving up on.

Brilliant wasn't going to believe it.

Tears flowed like rivers.

And she let them.

Showering with a baby monitor was new.

Mia had told him the twins were early risers, so Jordon was up before dawn taking care of his own morning routine so he'd be ready for the preschoolers when they awoke.

Normally, he gave himself a moment under the spray to wake up. Let the hot water loosen his muscles. Normally he shaved in the shower. That morning he was in and out in about a minute. Shaved at the sink—already dressed in the only other pair of shorts he had with him, tan ones, with a black polo shirt—and with his bathroom and bedroom doors open.

He'd had the twins' door open before they awoke. And was seated just outside at the dining table, scrolling on his phone.

They were in a strange room. And Mia's wasn't the first face they were going to see.

By the time they finally stirred, an hour later, he had several educationally fun shows for four-year-olds queued up and ready on his phone and hit play on the first, volume high as he entered the room.

Mariah O'Connell had talked about a lot of things in a very short period of time. Distraction was the one that had stuck.

Two shows later, the three of them were still sitting there, the girls in their jammies, propped up on the bed's headboard, watching shows.

Ruby and Violet were on one side of the phone he had propped up in the middle of the blanket. He was on the other.

It wasn't a daddy cuddling with his girls.

But it was close enough for him.

He could do this.

He could father his daughters.

He'd give it another day or two of thought and then, if he still felt that the decision was in the girls' best interests, he'd let Sierra's Web know that he'd be moving Violet and Ruby back to New York with him.

He'd go through the list the estate people were going to send him regarding things in the house, share it with Mia, make decisions and then Sierra's Web could handle the rest of the details regarding the estate. Including selling the house.

And they'd put all the funds in a trust for Ruby and Violet, to transfer to them when they turned twenty-one.

Until then, and through college, he'd support his daughters himself.

Assuming he decided to keep them.

Mia had a whole week's worth of videos planned— things she could shoot that evening after Jordon took the girls home to their cabin to bed—by the time Jordon texted to say he'd called down for breakfast to be sent up and asked her to join them.

He'd ordered her a ham, egg and cheese breakfast burrito with potatoes and onions as add-ons.

Something she hadn't had in a long while.

But that had been a favorite of hers during college.

And as they ate, he talked about taking the girls to the aquarium. She hadn't known there was one. Seemed kind of odd, aquatic animals in a desert, but what did she know?

"It's new to the city since I lived here," Jordon told her, his eyes aglow with a light she didn't know if she'd ever seen. Excitement, yes, but…more. "It's on the northeast side, up in or near Scottsdale," he continued, as though she knew the city well enough to travel mentally with him.

When she shrugged, because the day was up to him, he asked the girls if they wanted to see a dolphin. Started talking about the exhibits, and after they both gave enthusiastic yeahs, he looked to Mia again. With a smile that was filled with a bit of excitement, too, she nodded.

They'd be back at the ranch by dinner. With a completely fun day behind them.

A day of pleasure together that would be the start of their future?

She didn't let herself dwell on the thought. Set her sights on living every moment of the day, helping the girls smile and laugh their way through it, getting as many pictures as she could.

As they'd established the day before, she supervised Ruby's snapping herself into her car seat and Jordon oversaw Violet's do-it-yourself process. She couldn't help the wave of warmth that spread through her as she glanced over at him and found him looking at her.

Like parents, bonding over the heads of their children?

They'd both been poleaxed in the past week with a

circumstance that had changed them forever, and yet…
in handling the situation…they made a good team.

Mia had just buckled her own belt, and Jordon
had barely started his rented SUV in the hotel's covered garage, when Violet asked, "Are we going home
now?"

And Ruby immediately followed with, "Are we
going home?"

Turning, Mia looked at them both, saw them looking at her expectantly, and when Jordon didn't immediately respond said, "Where's home?"

Thinking that maybe bringing the girls back to
the city had been a little early in their moving-on
process.

"You know," Violet said, frowning.

Maybe they'd need to do a drive by at least.

And then see.

Looking over at him, she asked, "You've got the
key, right?"

His nod, his somewhat blank look, told her he
wasn't sure what to do. Such an odd thing, the way
the ten-years-older Jordon seemed to know less than
the college version had done.

"Are we going home?" Ruby asked again. "Macy
might miss us."

Wait. What?

"Macy?"

Violet nodded so big her chin touched her chest.
"'Cause we give her treats every morning."

"That's where you want to go?" Jordon asked then, glancing in the rearview mirror.

"Yeah!" both girls said in unison. "Home to see Macy!" Violet added.

And Jordon put the vehicle in gear. "Then that's where we'll go," he said, in a happy tone that was clearly meant for the young twins behind him.

"Yay!" Ruby said. Then asked, "How long until we get there?"

"How high can you count?" Jordon's reply was exactly what he'd asked the girls the day before every single time they'd asked the question on the way to Phoenix.

He didn't seem to mind. Didn't lose patience with their constant queries, even now that they weren't yet capable of calculating his response. He just got creative. Told them they'd be there in as long as it took two of their favorite pig cartoons to play. That they'd be there after two more people got to be with Macy.

And on it went.

He didn't seem bothered by the missed trip to see the dolphins.

Mia had no idea what kind of effect the day's plans change would have on the future, though. Her stomach knotted over the breakfast she'd consumed as she worried that he'd think the twins were already shrinking into introverts who were afraid to leave their comfort zones.

Funny how all the words and phrases he'd thrown at her that last night they were together in the past were coming out of storage. She'd thought she'd wiped them from her brain, when, instead, she'd just buried them.

And in that moment, she was glad they were there. A healthy reminder not to get her hopes up regarding anything Jordon said about a future that included her.

He didn't consider her lifestyle choices healthy ones.

And the signature on the girls' bottom line was all his.

They still hadn't gone through the boxes of the girls' things deposited in one of Mia's spare bedrooms.

On Sunday afternoon, when the girls were worn out from their time with Macy, followed by playing in the pool with new kids who'd just checked in and then insisting on time at the playground set in a fenced-off area in the middle of the cabins, Mia suggested a kids movie at her house. And Jordon, after seeing the girls lying down together on Mia's couch, their drooping eyelids facing the flat-screen television mounted to the wall, suggested that he and Mia go through the boxes.

He needed to know what to put in storage with whatever was coming out of the house for the girls, and what to move to the cabin.

He needed to stay busy. To be doing.

Because the weight of what to do for the girls' future was weighing on him.

They'd designated an area for things that were going into long-term storage, one for the girls' immediate use, and a third to be shipped to Ruby and Violet's permanent home.

His place, he was thinking.

But something was holding him back from fully committing to that end.

The long-term storage pile was easy: Madeline's and Keith's yearbooks, though why he'd brought them with him in the initial boxes, he didn't know.

When he started to put Madeline's jewelry in that pile as well, Mia shook her head. "You need to keep that with them, Jordon. Even if they don't know it's there. That's going to be intensely personal to them someday and shouldn't be in some storage unit someplace."

"Maybe a lockbox?" he asked, thinking of the one he had at the bank in New York, just a couple buildings down from his. The box had come free as part of his premium customer ranking when he'd made his first large deposit. It had been empty ever since.

"That's where I would put it," Mia was saying, opening the large box that contained all the stuffed animals he'd found in the girls' home. "And these would be good for you to take to the cabin with you. Like we talked about, introduce them now, and then let them take them to their permanent home…"

She didn't say his place. Or to New York.

And hadn't made any mention at all that day of

their talk the night before. His offer, his promise, to give her summers on the ranch with their daughters.

Her daughters, he amended, thinking of her comment to that end the night before. And his. Science.

Not a family.

Of course, with the girls in constant company there'd been little time for conversation of a serious, adult nature. But at the pool...

He'd sat alone while she'd talked to a couple of families who'd just checked in that day.

He'd noticed, though, that she'd kept an eye on the twins at all times, too. Always aware. That was the Mia he'd known and loved.

Past tense.

Please, fates. Past tense.

"Jordon?"

Standing there in the short denim skirt she'd had on all day, topped by a white sleeveless shirt that reminded him once again how well he knew the exact shape of her breasts, Mia was still holding the first two stuffed animals she'd pulled from the box. A purple unicorn and a white one.

Staring at him.

Right. The stuffed animals going with him to the cabin.

"The cabin's fine," he said, motioning to the box. "Just leave them packed and I'll carry the whole thing down. Maybe let the girls unpack them?"

She nodded but was still watching him.

And he reminded himself that, in some ways,

whether she knew it or not, Mia Jones knew him better than anyone ever had.

She knew how to read him.

Apparently, some things didn't change.

So…he'd give her what she seemed to want.

Mostly because he didn't know of any other way to proceed.

Chapter Fifteen

"You don't trust me."

Shock went through Mia when she first heard the words. Betrayal even. She and Jordon, they'd been existing under some kind of unspoken truce to just deal with the girls. Not each other.

She'd already told him she didn't trust him.

How could he...

But she knew.

He was right to face what she didn't want to acknowledge. Having the two of them as parents, sharing parenting duties, might not be best for Ruby and Violet in the long run.

She wanted to let anger take over.

Or persuasion.

But knew she wouldn't like herself if she did either.

"No, I don't," she said. But then words continued coming to her. "Not as far as I'm concerned. And yet, in a way, I do, in that I know what not to rely on. I know how you really feel now."

"You have no idea how I feel." Sounded a bit like he was letting anger do his talking. She waited a moment, but when he didn't continue, she did.

"I do trust you where the girls are concerned," she told him. "More than I'd trust anyone else." He needed to know that. "Even knowing how you feel about my life choices…and knowing that I could lose out… I trust you to do what you think is best for Ruby and Violet."

"What if what I think is best turns out not to be?"

She hadn't expected that. Had thought she was freeing him up to do what he was going to do.

And hope that the court gave her visitation rights if he took them away.

"You're doubting yourself?" she asked. And telling her about it?

"I want them."

She smiled then. The way he said it, with such fatherly ownership…

"So take them," she said, knowing that her girls would be well cared for. Watched over. Tended to. "Madeline and Keith had your dossier, Jordon," she reminded him. "They chose you. And really, the choice was theirs to make. They chose what they wanted for their daughters' futures. Your only decision, really, is whether or not you can honor their wishes. Whether or not you want those children. And it sounds as if you do."

She was babbling. But let the words pour out of her. Because they'd built up inside her, in the midst of all of the rest.

"They could have just left them for me to find them a good home."

"I'm guessing they'd have stated as such in their bequeathment if that's what they wanted from you."

He nodded, as though he'd already had the thought himself.

And then it occurred to her. "Is it that you aren't sure you really want them?"

"Oh, God, no." His response nearly brought tears to her eyes. He wanted their children. The babies that had grown from the embryos she'd talked him into making with her.

"Then what?" It was kind of nice. The two of them talking with each other. Like…normal. Rather than having shields drawn at all times.

"It's us."

"Us?" And just like that, her walls shot up. She wasn't in time to save her heart from harm. But she could hold on to her sanity. And to the part of her that would do anything for her children.

"You don't trust me."

Yeah, they'd already established that. She was done talking.

"You really think it's healthy for kids to be raised by parents who've already destroyed each other?"

Destroyed each other?

That was news to her.

What had she done to hurt him? She'd given him everything. Had been honest from the beginning...

"I really loved you, Mia. Deeply."

Her heart started to tear. She sewed it right back up.

"I loved you, too." Past tense. Dead now. He'd killed it.

"Just not as much as you loved Shelter Valley."

Her entire body froze. She couldn't draw air. Or even think for a second. She dropped to the bed, staring up at him.

"That's not true." He really didn't get it.

"It seemed that way to me."

"Jordon, people are just different. They can't help it. Introverts, they need what they need. Extroverts, the same. People who need sunshine to feel their happiest, and those who aren't affected by the weather one way or another. Those who can survive in the desert and those who dry out and die. People who relate to animals better than they do most people. And those who need a crowd around to be able to thrive. To breathe freely."

She'd just proven that she and Jordon had never been going to make it. Not ten years before. And no time in the future, either.

But...

What?

She could tell him she trusted him to make the decisions he thought best for their children and then try to convince him to do something he wasn't sure about.

The offer the night before…he'd made it because he knew it was what she wanted. Just like he'd always told her okay in the past.

And she knew what she had to do. "Take the girls to New York, Jordon. Start your life with them. And if the court gives me visitation rights, we can figure out how we go about making that work." Her insides crumbled, but sitting there, she didn't let it show.

She'd learned a lot in ten years.

And she had Brilliant just a few yards and a barn away.

Her heart might hurt like hell, but Jordon—life— wasn't going to break her again.

Jordon listened. Really listened. To what he thought Mia was saying.

And didn't feel any better.

"I don't want to do it without you, Mia. It feels… wrong. And not just in terms of you and me and you being the one who convinced me to donate and then you lose out on raising your own kids. But in terms of the girls, too. They're going to remember you. This week, Macy…you've helped them through what I hope turns out to be the toughest time of their lives. And when they get older, and find out that I'm their biological father, and want to know about their biological mother, and it's you…they deserve to know you."

Just as she deserved to know them.

The girls came first. Most definitely. But Mia mattered. A lot.

Too much?

Was he finding it so impossible to get around her because he didn't want to? Was his hesitation to take the girls because a part of him knew that he was doing it partially because he wanted Mia in his life, too?

Mia helping him along the way.

And he was only convincing himself of what was best for the girls in a way that fit his own scenario?

Like he'd done with Mia for four years?

"I'm confused." He'd seen her frown. Hadn't been sure he was ready for whatever was coming.

"Confused how?"

"You want me to be a part of things like you laid out last night?"

"Yes."

"Then…what…the bit about us not being healthy for the kids…"

He almost didn't want to say. In case he was saying it for the wrong reasons. His own selfish reasons.

"It can't be healthy for kids to be raised by two people who can't be real with each other. Who have so many defenses between them it's a wonder they can talk at all."

She seemed to consider his words, then said, "Or maybe it's better this way. As long as we keep our defenses in place, we can't hurt each other again.

Which means that things are always civil between us. The girls won't have to choose sides. Or even have a sense that there are sides. Because whatever differences we have, we work out without recrimination clouding the issues."

He didn't argue. But didn't feel convinced.

"The past is past, Jordon. An 'us' is gone. Has been for a long time. We've created great, successful lives without each other. Which means the future can be two people who made babies raising them. Ruby and Violet are all that we have in common."

Jordon wanted to argue with her. Didn't see a way for the pretty picture she was painting to work.

And didn't know how to tell her that he'd never be able to pretend that Ruby and Violet were all they had in common.

Mia was on a roll.

Thinking completely clearly for the first time in a week. Finally seeing how it was all going to work.

Until he said, "Except that every time I look at you, really look at you… I still find you attractive, Mia. Mega attractive. Like more attractive than any woman I've ever known. And in New York, I've…"

She held up her hand before he could complete a sentence that would be with her forever. "I get it, Jordon," she said.

And was without clarity again.

Completely. No more words.

But there was one beacon of knowledge. Blinding her with truth.

They had to deal with it.

"I find you just as gorgeous," she said, trying to maintain her hard-won ability to remain calm in all situations. "It's natural, don't you think, since the sex was so great between us?"

When his eyes grew smoky, his particular brand of hot, she flooded between her legs, her nipples perked into nubbins, and she said, "But it was so good because of the love we thought we shared." And knew there was truth there, too. "For me, the emotion is a huge part of sex, Jordon. More even than the body parts and how they look and what they do. Which means, for me, anyway, it won't be an issue. I might want you, but I know what I'm lusting after is an illusion. It's a memory that was built on a fantasy."

At least she hoped to God that was all it was.

She truly believed that was all it was.

"I need more than an assurance that sex won't be an issue," he said then, taking the wind out of her sails once again. He sat beside her, not touching her, but her body knew him.

Liked having him there.

"What do you need?" she asked because he was so close. And so much was at stake.

"I need to know that we can be at our best, together, for the girls. Because if they have me, they're going to need you. If not this year, then next, or the one after that. Or, the alternative, we give them to a two-parent couple in a healthy relationship."

Mia jumped up. She paced a minute. And when she felt like she was going to split in half, she blurted, "I need to use the restroom." She barely got the words out before she was out the door. Needing air.

Needing to peek in on Ruby and Violet.

The twins were sound asleep, cuddled up together on the couch.

And the movie still had a way to go.

She didn't want to go back to Jordon. She wanted to be in a stall. Visiting with Brilliant until she had her zen back.

But if she couldn't have a tough conversation with Jordon, how could she possibly be good for her daughters?

Two things occurred almost simultaneously, then. She turned back toward her spare room littered with boxes and piles.

And she knew what she was going to say when she got there.

Because one thought of the girls made it happen.

"Okay, here's what I can promise you. I'll do anything to bless those babies' lives," she said, standing in the doorway. "I love them that much. I think about them, and suddenly I have a strength I didn't know I had. And my own emotions—it's like they lose power in favor of their little hearts. And minds. And well-being. I'm guessing it's a mother's instinct, but I have no basis of proof for that."

That was it. Everything she had. Right there.

Jordon stood. His intent stare never leaving her gaze.

The future lay there in that gaze.

She waited to see what it would bring.

"I feel exactly the same way," he said. "It's the most bizarre thing…this feeling. These girls have me in their grips. Fatherhood. Not anything I thought I absolutely had to have. And yet, here I am. I'd run into a burning house for those two. Jump in front of a train for them. Whatever it takes, to be at my best, to give them my best…"

Tears filled her eyes.

Maybe they filled his, too. She couldn't see clearly enough to know.

But she knew one thing.

She and Jordon had finally shared a set of vows.

And they were promises she trusted both of them to keep.

Chapter Sixteen

They were doing it.

And they weren't.

Elation warred with trepidation, common sense, details and bone-deep regret, too, as Jordon drove in the dark to get to his hotel suite in time for the morning bell on Monday. He'd left a sleepy Mia behind on her porch as he'd run out the door at her approach, handing off the baby monitor as he headed for the SUV.

Which dug up another confusion of emotion.

He was going to keep his daughters.

The thought scared the hell out of him.

And energized him in a way he'd never imagined. Who knew that life had this whole incredibly complex and invigorating dimension that he hadn't even known existed? Why hadn't his friends with kids told him?

Friends…work associates, really. Ones he trusted and socialized with.

When they weren't with their families.

Or when it was a "just adults" gathering and he had a date along.

Dating.

The word crossed his mind.

No time or interest in pursuing a thought about it.

Mia.

She loomed hugely on his horizon. Just that. Loomed.

He couldn't do it without her. Not morally. Not emotionally.

But couldn't let himself get involved with her, either. Not personally.

So…looming.

Moving the girls to New York.

His apartment was larger than a lot of places in Manhattan. No problem there.

Furniture.

Needed to order.

Sooner rather than later so it was there when he and the girls arrived. Arrangements to be made to get it set up in his absence.

Six names came immediately to mind.

All six people he'd be seeing virtually, one-on-one, later that morning.

He was a father.

Had daughters.

Brown Eyes and Blue Eyes.

In a few years, they were...

Nope. Not going there.

Too much to worry about in the present.

Everyone was going to be shocked.

Might even think he couldn't do it.

Could he do it?

Seriously...him.

His lifestyle.

No more going out most nights.

He waited for the disappointment to hit. The caged feeling.

He'd have power lunches.

The city came to life most during the warmer months. He'd be free every night during the summer.

Maybe become the guy who was seen out and about with his twins.

Yeah, he liked that thought a lot.

People were going to scoff. Him? They wouldn't believe it.

Ma.

Damn. He pushed the phone button on the steering wheel, waited for the beep and said, "Call Ma on cell."

And noticed his palms were sweating.

Like he was jumping off the bridge once and for all.

Taking the dive of his life.

"Jordie? It's been six days and I haven't heard from you."

Brows raised, he glanced at the dash screen, checking that he'd connected right.

Ma. And the number was right, too.

"I...don't usually call every day," he reminded, still trying to decipher the odd note in her tone. Not anger. Or even recrimination.

But something more than the placid sounds that always came from her.

"What did you decide, Jordie?"

And, again, he felt like he took a brick to the head. What was it with him? Failing to see how his actions and words affected others?

"Until late last night, nothing for sure, Ma. I'd have called if I had." He'd have bet his life she'd have known that.

"I know, Jordie." Her tone quieted. And then she said, "I just...this is..."

She cared. A lot.

The idea energized him again.

"Mia and I talked last night," he told her, a bit more enthused to share his news. If his mother did think he was making a mistake, as he'd somewhat expected, then he'd just have to prove her wrong. She'd said she'd help, and...

"And? Are you giving her the children?"

"No, Ma, I'm bringing them home. For the school years. They'll spend summers with Mia on the ranch."

No response.

None.

"Ma?"

"Yeah." She sounded...deadpan. Like he, his information, wasn't even important enough to yield a reaction?

"You said you'd help, Ma. Did you mean that?"

"What?" A brief pause and then, "Oh, yes, Jordie, of course!" Her tone sounded odd. Maybe excited. Definitely distracted.

What the hell?

She didn't trust him, either? Didn't believe that he was going to do what he said he'd do?

She'd never said...

"Ma?"

"Mmm-hmm?"

"Ma!"

"What?" Definite alarm entered her tone then.

"Are you hearing what I'm saying here?"

"Oh, yes, Jordie!"

"You don't sound like it."

"I'm just...hold on..." He held. Breathing harder than normal. If he didn't know better, he'd think she was confused or something.

Then it hit him, maybe she had someone there. Someone she didn't want him to know about?

"I'm sorry, Jordie, I'm here. And yes, I'll help you! Anything you need, son, anytime."

Babysitting.

Bing. The answer had been right there all along. His mother was family.

The girls would be with family when he had to be gone.

But… "What were you just doing?" What was so important she'd been blowing him off?

"Making my flight reservation."

"Your flight?" She was taking a trip? Right when he was bringing the girls home? She never took trips. She talked about them, but she never took them.

"Yes."

"You just booked a flight."

"Yes."

"Where?"

"Phoenix."

"Phoenix." She was coming to him? She never ever came to him. Not when he was a kid, unless he'd called and asked. Then she was there. Every time.

"I'm coming home, Jordie. Today. I can't wait another minute to meet my granddaughters. I've been waiting all week, watching flights, hardly able to sleep…"

Her words dropped off, almost as if she'd just heard herself. Jordon wished she'd continued jabbering.

It was…refreshing.

Nice.

All except the *home* part. What was that?

"You just booked a flight to Phoenix for today?"

He needed her to keep talking to buy him some time to figure out what he was going to do with his mother in a two-bedroom cabin.

Or at Mia's place at all.

Mia had just agreed to co-parent with him. They'd work together.

There'd be hardships. Bumps in the road. They hadn't said so, but the knowledge had been there between them.

But he sure hadn't expected one so soon. How did he ask Mia to coexist with her ex's mother when she still wasn't all that proficient at dealing with said ex?

How did he tell her he was taking the girls to the suite after all, rather than leaving them on the ranch during the day?

How did he take his girls away from Macy when he'd just told them they had another week there?

Thoughts flew so fast he hardly noticed that silence hung on the line. Wasn't sure how much time had passed.

"What time's your flight, Ma?"

"There!" Her voice came over the line. "I just got my boarding pass," she told him, obviously unaware that he'd just been spit out from a cyclone of panic. "I land at three thirty your time, Jordie," she said. "Now don't worry about me. I'm booking my room next. There's a nice new hotel not far from Gloria's apartment. And I'll get a cab."

Gloria Baron. Their next-door neighbor from long ago. She'd been out to stay with Layla a time or two.

"I'll come pick you up, Ma," he said, not at all sure how he was going to wing everything that was coming at him.

Layla in a hotel that night would be good, at least. Give her time to catch up with her friend.

And give him the chance to prepare Mia for the next potentially painful moments she was going to have to face in order to share parenting with him. He'd be taking the girls with him when he left the ranch in the morning.

For once, just once, couldn't he arrive on her doorstep with no pain involved?

Mia had the best day ever. Partially because she had the girls to herself—or rather, was their only parent—for the first time in two days. And a lot because she was finally starting to let herself believe that she was going to get to mother her children for the rest of her life.

Mostly, though, it was because Ruby and Violet were hilarious and sweet and loving and needy and precocious and innocent and a little naughty sometimes and she never knew what was going to be coming out of their mouths. She'd burst out with laughter. Or tear up at the profoundness.

And because she was now in for life, she let it happen. Let herself experience it all fully.

She thought about calling Lincoln and Sara. Letting her siblings know that there were two more children in the family to guard and love and spoil.

But she wasn't ready to deal with their reaction to her agreement with the twins' father. She and Jordon needed a little time to themselves, to sort out the overall parameters of exactly how they were going to make their situation work, to figure out how to deal with each other, before getting family involved.

She shuddered to think about Lincoln and Jordon in the same room together. Certainly didn't want the girls around for that first meeting.

She didn't even want to be there for it.

Testosterone overload to the max.

Between her brother and the father of her children. No, thank you.

Mia was particularly relieved she'd held off the temptation to notify her family about her most major life change when, later that Monday evening, Jordon texted and asked if she could come down to the cabin for a bit.

When she left her office, saw him sitting outside in one of the cabin's two wooden chairs on the small deck off the living room, she got a sinking feeling in her stomach.

He had the baby monitor.

But none of the girls' things were there. Not the cowboy boots they'd already learned to take off before going inside. Not the swimsuits she'd left drying on the rail.

Could be that Jordon had become a clean freak during their ten years apart, but one flash of his hotel room over the weekend put that hope to death.

By the time she reached him, sinking had turned to sick. Knotted and sick.

His face didn't look any more welcoming than the barren porch.

"What?" she asked him, keeping her tone low in deference to the other cabins situated around the grounds.

She could hear a child counting loudly, as though playing hide and seek. Giggling. A television.

And tried to take them in, focus on them.

On families having fun.

"I couldn't tell her no, Mia."

Jordon's words hit her. He'd been speaking, softer even than she'd done, and she'd missed his first words.

Tell who no?

One of the girls?

She'd seen them for dinner. Grilled hamburgers at the cabin. A Jordon surprise. Ruby had eaten a whole one. Violet almost had. Both girls had been busy, taking bites and then running off from the outdoor picnic table to explore something one of them found in the dirt. Or to watch kids from the next cabin playing hide and seek.

"I'm sorry," she said. "Tell who no about what?"

"My mother's in Phoenix."

She stared. Felt her face grow stiff. Layla Lawrence had been like a mother to her.

Once upon a time.

In fairy-tale land.

"I don't understand."

"I told her about the girls."

So much for them parenting together. She'd held off notifying her family, and without even telling her, he'd told his.

"When?"

"Last week."

That long ago. The fact that he hadn't shared that news with her hurt. Far more than it should have done.

She'd talked to Lincoln. He'd known that Jordon's kids were staying at her place. She hadn't told Jordon that her brother had called.

But she also hadn't told her brother that Jordon's kids were at the ranch. Nor had she told them that the twins were hers, too.

Crushing disappointment continued to reverberate through her. Blocking coherent thought while she sat with the pain.

"Did you tell her that you were keeping them then, too?"

It shouldn't matter.

But it did.

She'd thought that she and Jordon had been alone in their private world the whole past week. Adjusting to the shock of being parents together, first, before telling anyone else close to them.

"I told her I was thinking about it."

Something he hadn't told Mia until just a couple of days before. It was clear that his loyalty did not lie with her.

And there was no reason it should. He owed her nothing.

She'd just fallen right back into her trap from the past. Believing what she needed to believe, blinding her to what was really there.

She nodded. Wished the chair rocked.

Or that she could get off it and head to the barn.

To her office.

To a glass of wine in the tub.

But she had her daughters to think of.

Even if he was about to take them from her.

Layla had come through. Could easily replace his immediate need for Mia.

There was still the court ruling to hope for.

And so…she sat.

Chapter Seventeen

"She made the reservations before I even knew what she was doing." Jordon got out what he considered to be the most important point for the moment. "Today," he added. "She just made them today."

"Why today?" Mia's calm was unnerving. Her question holding mere curiosity, like she was talking to a stranger.

Making it clear to him that he was a stranger to her.

Panicked all over again, fighting back the debilitating doubts that he couldn't afford, he sat forward. Trying to figure out what to say to get her to like him again. Even a little bit.

And came up with nothing but the truth.

Between him and Mia, for him, it would be only the truth until the day he died. "Because I called her this morning to tell her that we were keeping the girls."

"We?" Her head cocked. The *we* had hit a chord.

A good one or a bad one? He couldn't read her.

Was attacked by a frustration surge.

"Of course, we."

"Does she know that we aren't a couple?"

He hadn't specifically said so. But…

"Yes," he said. "I told her that I'd have the girls during the school year and that they'd be spending summers on the ranch with you."

Her lips seemed a little less thin. Could be he was just imagining that. Seeing what he wanted to see.

"And then she just arbitrarily decided to fly out?"

He'd known Mia wouldn't welcome the tension of having his mother around. He hadn't expected the height of the walls the news would put between them.

Another something he wasn't seeing, he was sure.

Didn't help him deal with the fallout any.

Most particularly because he hadn't even given her the bad news.

"Yeah," he said, and, because he didn't want to get into the rest of what he had to tell her, he went another direction. One he'd have taken in the past.

"It's odd, Mia," he said. "You know how she was always so…distant…"

"Your mother was never distant, Jordon. She just gave you your space."

Throwing his hands up, nodding, he gave her that.

"But her whole bearing…she just takes stuff, doesn't get worked up about any of it. Good or bad."

"I always admired that about her," Mia said. And he stared. Mia had talked to his mom. He'd never asked what about. Women talked.

But looking at her, watching her calm…even as her instant distance had told him he'd triggered something in her…had Layla taught her that? And he just hadn't seen the change happening back then?

"She didn't used to be that way," he told her then. "It happened after my father died. I've always thought that a part of her died with him."

He'd never told anyone that before. About a part of his mother dying.

Maybe not even, consciously, himself.

Darkness had fallen, earlier than in New York, as it did in Arizona. He'd forgotten that until the past week.

Had forgotten so many things.

Like the way Mia's hair seemed to speak a language of its own. Enticing him with its messiness, even as it warned that she wouldn't be messed with.

Intriguing him with character that was all Mia, though he knew he could no longer run his fingers through it.

"She was pretty chill," Mia was saying, as he stared at her hair. Trying not to feel any of the emotions trying to slam through him. At least Mia was talking to him. "I just thought she was always that way."

Because he'd never talked to her about the way his life had changed after his father died. In college, he'd been all about his studies, his buddies, her and the future.

He shook his head then. To rid himself of the dust coming from disturbed cobwebs. And to disavow her last statement, too.

"That's the thing," he said, leaning forward, hoping he could help her understand why he was allowing a third party to descend upon them before they'd had a chance to even figure out how "them" was going to work.

"Last week, when I called her to tell her I couldn't make our weekly dinner because I was in Phoenix..."

"...you have weekly dinner with your mom?"

Her shock should have surprised him. Sadly, it didn't. He'd put off gatherings with his mother when he and Mia had been in college. Finding all kinds of excuses to do so.

"I do," he told her. "Every Tuesday."

When she said nothing more, he continued, "I had to tell her why I was in Phoenix and, for a second there...it was weird. She started, almost grilling me. At least more of a grill than she's done since I was about the girls' age."

The girls. Their girls.

Their daughters.

The magnitude of having kids hit him once again. Filling him so full of emotions, he didn't know what to do with any of it. And that they were also Mia's...

He took a breath. Got himself back on track. "Then today, she was like this woman I didn't even know. All full of...just full. No way I could suck any of that out of her."

"You think it's because of Ruby and Violet?" Mia's tone had softened. And he thought about just letting her go to bed thinking that Layla's visit was all he'd had to tell her that night.

She'd figure out the rest. As soon as she had time to think about logistics. But if they could just say good-night on a good note...

"I do," he told her.

And she smiled. An honest, full of goodness Mia smile.

"Where is she now?" Mia was frowning again.

He told her about the arrangements Layla had made before telling him she was coming. About the hotel by Gloria's place.

Was building up to the point where he told her that he'd be taking the girls with him to the city in the morning, knowing that her next question was going to involve Layla meeting her granddaughters, when Mia said, "She has to come back with you tomorrow night, Jordon. I have a family of only three who wanted a two-bedroom place, but I didn't have any available. I'm sure they'll switch with you. And even if they won't, I have plenty of room, as you well know. She can stay at the house..."

He stared.

"You want my mother here?"

"Of course! She was wonderful to me, almost like a mother sometimes…" Coming from a woman who'd lost her own mother to a bizarre strike of lightning when she was not much older than Violet and Ruby, Jordon could hardly believe what he was hearing.

He'd known the two got along. Well.

But Mia had never said…

Or he'd never listened?

How did he know?

It was all so long ago…

"You haven't seen her in ten years." Someone had to see that his thinking wasn't all backward. If Mia had cared so deeply about his mother, why hadn't she stayed in touch?

"She's your mother, Jordon. The only family you had. There was no way I was going to put her in the middle of us…"

No way she was going to tell his mother he'd lied to her for four years. Or let Layla see how badly he'd broken her heart.

"Or tell her that you loved Shelter Valley more than you loved me."

The words fell out of him again. Shaming him.

But he wasn't the only bad guy in their situation. Yeah, he'd been a bit full of himself in college. And he'd lacked certain…perspective.

But he'd truly loved Mia.

And the look on her face told him he'd gone too far. Trespassed where they'd agreed not to go in order to make parenting work in a healthy manner for their daughters. "I'm sorry," he said. And then, before she could take back the offer that was going to let everyone continue on in a positive form for a few more days at least, he said, "And if you're sure you don't mind, I will most definitely bring Ma here tomorrow after work."

Mia studied him for a second, her eyes glowing by one of the many security lights keeping campers safe in the desert, and then said, "Good."

That was it. Just good.

But she didn't get up and leave. Or walk out without a good-night, which had kind of become their habit as of late.

She talked about making a nice dinner for all of them. About letting the girls introduce his mother to Macy. And show her their crafts.

"Thank you," Jordon said when she finally fell silent.

"For what?" She was looking him in the eye again.

For being you, he wanted to say. Couldn't make it that personal. "For welcoming my mother into your home. I know it's not going to be easy."

With a shrug, she didn't deny the awkwardness. The painful memories and lost dreams that being with his mother might engage. "She's their grandmother, Jordon," she whispered. "The only one they're going to have. They need her. And they're lucky to have her."

Reminding him that one of the things that had

bonded the two of them early on, was the way they'd both grown up in similar circumstance. Coming from a one-parent home, having lost a parent to death, and having no grandparents.

"They're lucky to have you, too," he told her then.

And had to look away before he made the moment between them very personal.

She had to leave.

Danger loomed all over the porch. In the air. The scents. The sounds. Because all of them seemed to encase her and Jordon into their own little world.

But she couldn't go yet.

She had a motherly duty that had just been pushed to the forefront.

"When are we going to tell the girls that we're their parents?"

Mariah O'Connell had suggested that Jordon do so as soon as he decided to keep them. But only if he decided to do so. She'd read the report.

"Four-year-olds aren't going to understand biology," she quoted from the child life specialist's advice. "They won't need to know details, or that we're their biological parents, until they're older."

"We're their new parents," he said, nodding. He'd read the report, too, she knew.

"Ones who don't live together," she added quickly, when the air got too thick. And then moved on to her destination. "We can't introduce your mother as their new grandmother until they know we, or at least you, are their parent."

"We," Jordon said, sounding almost irritated with her.

Bringing on the urge for her to smile again. She didn't. But she savored that one word. Spoken as though he didn't like being doubted.

Like her being in the girls' lives really did matter to him.

A lot.

But there were other matters at hand.

Ones she'd been considering on and off all day.

With Jordon's decision made, and them having finished going through the girls' boxes...with his having hired the estate company, he had no more reason to stay.

Would he be taking the girls with him? Or...since it was summer for another few weeks at least, did they stay with her while he went back and got his life in New York ready for them?

He'd have people to notify, furniture to buy...

"We'll tell them tomorrow, before I head to Phoenix. I'll stay here until they wake up in the morning. Do what I can from my phone..."

"You're welcome to use my computer..." Thoughts were flying swiftly. "I'll come over in the morning, sit with the girls, and you can work in my office. When they get up, I'll get them bathed and dressed and then bring them up to the house for breakfast."

She was taking over. Could hear herself doing it. Was ready to be vetoed. Rightfully so.

"We can tell them over breakfast," Jordon said, nodding. Sounding pleased.

And so was she.

Smiling, she glanced at him.

He looked back at her.

And she got up and left.

The porch.

But turned before she made it past the stairs.

"Good night," she told him. Feeling better for having done so.

"Night, Mia," he said back.

And she let the Jordon-ness in his voice infiltrate her personal space a little bit.

Chapter Eighteen

Jordon was a nervous mess when Mia texted the next morning to let him know that breakfast was ready.

He'd heard the three of them come in, heard Mia tell the girls that they could watch a show on TV, but that they had to be quiet because Jordon was working in her office.

Until the text, though, he'd been able to focus fully on the activity on her computer screen. Including a couple of windows with private conversations taking place. People who worked for him.

People he trusted.

Then the text hit and he had to excuse himself.

From men and women who didn't yet know that he was a father.

"Look, Jordon! Mama Mia maked cheesy eggs!"

Violet proclaimed, wiggling on her knees on her seat at the table while she waved an arm in front of her as though unveiling a rare diamond instead of a steaming bowl of eggs.

The drama amused him. And made him fall in love all over again, too.

Every time.

Both twins were bursting with boatloads of the stuff.

As far as he was concerned, they could keep it coming until the day he died.

But something else hit him.

Jordon.

Mama Mia.

She was already Mama.

He was…just Jordon.

What if that was all they wanted him to be? They'd spent a week establishing a new normal. And…he reminded himself as he sat down…preschoolers didn't generally understand the concept of time because it was an abstract entity. According to both Mariahs.

When Mia sat, he sent her a look.

She didn't respond. Just served up eggs, giving the girls spoons, and put some cut-up bananas and strawberries on the little plates, too.

He waited to see if she was going to eat because he sure didn't feel like it. When she spooned up her own eggs, and took a bite, he did the same.

For about two seconds.

"Mama Mia, do you have something to tell the girls?" he blurted, feeling hot and cold at the same time.

"I sure do," Mia said, sounding excited, but still not making eye contact with Jordon. He needed her and...

Needing her wasn't part of their deal. Wasn't how it was going to work.

Needing her meant trouble down the road, which would then reverberate to Ruby and Violet. He and Mia had had the discussion. Had decided.

Both girls were busy eating, clearly more interested in breakfast than any adult news.

"Hey, Ruby, you want to know a secret?" Mia asked then.

The little blonde looked up, nodding, while, also on her knees, she took another bite of eggs.

"I want to know, too," Violet said. She stopped eating to look at Mia.

"Jordon has a new name, and only you get to use it."

"Only us?" Ruby's nose scrunched as she asked the question, her little voice ending on a higher, questioning note.

"Yep."

"What is it?" Violet's head spun to Jordon, along with a little spatter of egg, as the girl asked the question.

He was about to choke when Mia said, "It's Jordon Daddy, kind of like Mama Mia."

"Except now, you can just call us Mama and Daddy for short." He was breathing again. Had taken up the reins.

He was a father.

"Huh?" Violet, her whole face seeming to frown, swung her gaze to Mia, and Mia didn't panic. She nodded.

And words came to her.

"When mommies and daddies die, then sometimes kids get new mommies and daddies, and that's what happened. Only it's a little bit different because Jordon Daddy and Mama Mia don't live together in the same house…"

"…but we both love you as much as the whole sky," Jordon said from his end of the table, and Mia was thankful for him. He'd given them a tangible quantity. The sky was something they could see. And it never ended or went away.

The sky hadn't been in Mariah O'Connell's report.

"We don't have a died mommy and daddy, we have you?" Ruby asked, then looked to Violet.

"Yeah, we have you?" Violet looked between Mia and Jordon.

Blinking back tears, Mia said, "Yep!" She didn't ask if it was okay. While they needed to give the girls as many choices of their own to make as they could, she couldn't give them a choice that wasn't theirs to make.

Violet took a bite of egg. Ruby tried to scoop a banana slice with her spoon, failed, and picked the slice up with her fingers and shoved it into her mouth.

"Hey, um, guys…" Violet said, looking between Mia and Jordon again. "Do we still get to see Macy today and do swimming?" Her little-girl enunciation didn't distract from her seriousness.

"Yes." Mia nodded. And when both girls looked at Jordon, he nodded, too.

"Yay!" both girls called.

And then Ruby asked, "Can I be done eating now?" She'd cleaned her plate.

Violet quickly spooned up the last of her eggs and grabbed pieces of strawberry in each hand. "Can I be done, too?" she asked, her mouth full.

"What do you say?" Jordon asked, when Mia would have just let them off the hook, given the circumstances.

"Please?" the girls said in unison.

And Jordon granted them leave.

Mia was up, clearing away dishes before the girls were out of the room.

"That went well," Jordon said, joining her by the sink with his plate and the empty egg bowl. He was close enough for her to feel his heat.

And inhale the clean musky scent of him.

Before he was gone again.

And she was in the kitchen all alone.

Jordon waited until the final bell rang before leaving Mia's office. Just made sense, rather than losing more floor time on the drive. He'd texted Mia. She'd agreed.

And after a satisfactory day's work, he walked out into a completely silent house.

Mia had texted that the girls were going to try bareback riding, if he wanted to come out. He did want to, and noticed, as he let himself actually look around long enough to take in his surroundings, that the home felt completely different than it had in the past.

As a college student, he'd visited often, and the place had seemed…darker. Not as bright. Or open.

Yet, the same china hutch stood in the dining room, the key rack by the door hadn't changed, specific things he remembered were there.

The furniture? He couldn't be sure. He just remembered the hutch because Mia had cried when she'd once pulled out a dish and dropped it. He'd told her it was no big deal. They'd just get another one.

It had been her grandmother's and irreplaceable to her.

And the key rack…he'd felt like the tallest man alive the day he'd walked in and Mia's father had invited him to hang his keys on that rack.

He'd been accepted as one of them.

The old man had trusted him with his daughter's heart.

Jordon ripped his gaze away from that rack, bugged out and, ignoring the dirt getting on his dress shoes, strode with purpose over dusty ground toward the barn and corral behind it.

His purpose: escape the past he couldn't change and get to the future stretching out before him. And there they were.

Ruby and Violet, each with a single blond braid down their backs, with matching T-shirts, jeans and little cowboy boots, were astride horses being led by one woman in between them.

Mia.

None of them noticed him standing there at the fence, out of place in his expensive navy pants, and white dress shirt.

They were all glowing, bursting with something that he wasn't sure he'd ever felt before.

Yep, there they were.

The three people who'd changed his life forever.

For a second there, he was an observer to their joy, not only in what they were doing, but in doing it together. He panicked.

Couldn't see a place for himself in their lives.

"Jordon Daddy, look at me!" Violet had glanced his way. "Mama Mia says I can wide!"

"Yeah, wook at me!" Ruby called next.

Stepping completely up to the fence, leaning over it, he called back, "Great job!"

His glance stopped at Mia briefly, as he looked from one of his daughters to the other, but she didn't give him a chance to share a smile with her.

The moment was his.

And hers.

With the girls, separately.

He got it.

And knew his place, too.

There *were* three women who'd changed his life forever.

He'd already failed one of them.

He would not fail the other two.

Layla Lawrence was the one person in the world who knew how much Mia had loved Jordon. Others had guessed. Figured. Suspected. Layla was the only person, other than Jordon, Mia had ever told.

All day long, between soaking up moments with the girls, constantly aware that Jordon could be hauling them off to New York within a day or two, she tried to picture how the meeting with Layla would go.

How did you meet your ex's mother for the first time in ten years and pretend that you hadn't once felt like she was your mother, too?

Time passed. Memories…emotions…did not.

As she was learning about Layla's son.

She didn't trust Jordon. Couldn't be in a personal relationship with him. But she still loved him. On some level, she'd known the previous week.

Had finally admitted the truth to herself the night before.

Sitting there on the porch of a cabin she owned and he occupied.

Layla had reached out to her the week after Jordon left Arizona. And a couple of times after that as well.

Mia hadn't responded.

Hadn't been able to open her heart and reach out to anyone.

Until her father came home with Brilliant.

By the time she'd healed enough, found her own inner strength and set out to forge a new future for herself, she'd felt like too much time had passed to answer Layla's texts.

And had also decided, rightfully so she still thought, that it wasn't right to pull Jordon's mother in any direction that would take her away from her son. Even just not being able to mention her. Or have them both over for dinner.

Layla was the only family Jordon had.

At the time, Mia had still had her father.

And Lincoln and Sara and their spouses. Her nephew had been on the way.

Jordon had been living on a shoestring in New York and she'd had a ranch coming to her.

None of which mattered.

Layla wasn't coming to see Mia.

She was a grandmother on a mission to meet her granddaughters.

But no matter how many times Mia reminded herself of the facts, she couldn't stop the emotions swirling inside her.

She'd loved Layla. Was looking forward to seeing her.

And dreading it, too.

As it turned out, when she saw Jordon's SUV head up the long drive and took the girls out on the porch to wait for him, she didn't have to focus on keeping it about the twins. It just was.

"Come on, Jordon Daddy," Violet called from the porch as soon as Jordon stepped his first foot from the vehicle. "Mama Mia says chocolate milkshakes for tissert, but first we has to wait for dinner and you!"

Mia caught a glimpse of Jordon's smile as both girls, in matching short outfits from the wardrobe Jordon had brought from their previous home, ran down to hurry him up.

And then she looked over to the side of the car less visible to her. Saw the top of the door as it opened.

And then watched the blond hair appear. It was still long. Wavy.

She waited for the eyes. Blue like Jordon's.

But they weren't focused on her at all.

Layla Lawrence had a sparkle Mia had never seen before. Energy to her step as she rounded the car. And a gaze for no one but the little girls who were about to get very lucky.

Mia quietly tucked herself inside the house.

And kept her mostly happy tears to herself.

Chapter Nineteen

With his attention on his daughters and mother, eager for them to meet, Jordon still saw Mia slip away.

He missed her immediately.

And focused on his mother coming around the car, reaching an arm out to the slender, well-dressed blonde woman who'd always just been "Mom" to him. A woman he'd taken for granted, and perhaps hadn't really seen, for most of his life.

"Ruby, Violet, we have someone very special having dinner with us," he said, as the girls stopped dancing around as soon as they saw the stranger in their midst. Standing side by side, so close they were touching, both girls hung back, watching as Layla joined him.

He was ready to give her her name. Grandma. But

she stepped forward, squatting down in front of the twins.

"Oh, baby girls, I've been so excited to know you!" Layla's voice had the sound again. The one he'd heard on the phone.

"Now, I think you're Ruby...and you're Violet," Layla said, looking directly at the girls. She was close, but not in their faces. As though she knew exactly how to put uncertain four-year-olds at ease.

The girls both nodded. He'd told his mother about the differing eye color, only in a matter of relaying that he hadn't even known their names at first— hadn't expected her to remember who was who.

"You know what a grandmother is?" Layla asked next.

Wow. He'd told her in the car that the girls didn't know about her. That they'd only just told them that morning that he and Mia were Mama and Daddy.

Both girls nodded slowly, wide-eyed, as they watched her.

"Like Gran, on *The Little Mouse's House*," Ruby said, naming a show that he'd seen Mia turn on for the twins.

"That's right!" Layla, still down on her haunches, looked between the two of them. "And I'm your new grandma and you can call me Gran."

For a woman who'd stood back his entire life, leaving Jordon to forge his own way, the change in Layla was pretty staggering.

And...nice.

In an overwhelming kind of way.

He hadn't told her he'd planned to have the kids call her Grandma. Or even figured out himself exactly how he'd introduce her. He'd kind of assumed Mia would be involved and help out.

And there it was, done.

Or…not quite…he amended as Violet said, "Does Mama Mia say it's okay?"

Cringing for his mother's sake, afraid the newly found essence of joy emanating from Layla would fade away, Jordon opened his mouth to save the moment, but Layla was once again ahead of him.

"I don't know," she said, holding out a hand to each of the girls. "Why don't we go and find out?"

The girls took her hands. But didn't move.

Looking at him, Ruby said, "Is Jordon Daddy coming, too?"

"Of course," he answered before he'd had a coherent thought. And, with a hand resting gently on each of his daughters' backs, he followed them, and his mother, into Mia's house.

A place that had once felt like home to him.

But one in which he was no longer welcome except as his daughters' father.

Only because she'd been listening for it, Mia heard the front door open a split second before a small voice called out, "Mama Mia!"

And the other one, Ruby, she knew, called, "Mama Mia, look what we got!"

"It's a grandma!" Violet said then, bursting into the kitchen, Layla just half a step in tow behind her.

"Can we call her Gran?" Ruby asked then, her sweet face so dramatically serious as she stared up at Mia. "Pwetty pwease?"

"Yeah," Violet said then. "Pwetty pwease?"

She'd have granted the wish regardless, but with those sweet faces peering up at her, Mia granted immediate permission.

While the girls dropped Layla's hands to join their own and dance in a circle, singing tunelessly, "We got a Gran, we got a Gran," Mia's gaze met Layla Lawrence's for the first time in ten years.

"It's good to see you," she uttered the understatement. Layla looked amazing. Like herself, only younger, if that was possible with the passage of years. Dressed in vivid blue that matched her eyes, instead of the grayish shades she used to wear, her shoulders straight rather than hunched with worry, the woman's gaze swam with emotion.

"Can I have a hug, sweetie?" Layla asked, and Mia fell against her naturally. Held on for a long moment.

When she pulled away, Mia said, "I'm so sorry I didn't answer your texts…"

As the girls circled the kitchen, hands still joined, cries of "We get chocolate milkshakes," filling the room, Mia heard Layla say, "I understood, Mia. I didn't expect a response. I just wanted you to know you were still in my heart."

A sound to her left drew Mia's gaze. Not a cough. Or a snort.

Maybe a sharply indrawn breath.

She glanced over at Jordon, saw a shroud of pain cross his face, right before he dove into the girls' circle, picked them both up, one on each shoulder, and, acting like a galloping horse with sounds and all, took them into the living room.

And Mia, with Layla's help, got dinner on the table.

Layla wanted to give the girls their baths and read them their bedtime story. She'd said as much to Jordon when she suggested that he stay and help Mia with the cleanup after dinner.

He'd agreed because it was the right thing to do.

And because he wanted a few minutes alone with Mia. Just to make certain that things were good between them.

She was so good at keeping up appearances—something she'd perfected since he'd last known her—that he seemed to be in a constant state of not sure, where she was concerned.

And he needed to be sure.

Needed to know that he wasn't steering things the way he wanted them to go, assuming that in the end she'd be happiest.

He'd given up assuming where she was concerned.

And where Layla was, too, he amended, having just left his mother and the girls at the cabin when she made it clear that she didn't need his help getting her granddaughters ready for bed. She'd been sitting on the floor of their bedroom at the cabin, looking at the array of stuffed animals the twins were introducing to her.

His mother, sitting on the floor, suggesting that they braid a unicorn's mane.

Layla? On the floor? Guiding playtime instead of bedtime?

If he wasn't a grown man, and beyond petty selfishness, he'd have thought that she loved those two darlings she'd just met more than she'd ever loved him.

As it was, he flooded with love for her. Thankful that she adored Ruby and Violet.

And told her he was going for a walk.

Mia had declined his offer to help clean up after dinner.

But he was going back.

He'd received the list from the estate company that afternoon. It was long, generated by several employees who'd each taken two rooms of the pristinely cleaned house. He intended to send the list to Mia later that night but wanted to talk to her about how they were going to proceed from there before he did so.

His plan, to keep a master copy on the cloud and both work off from that, making notes for each other as needed, with basic designations for things, similar to what they'd done with their piles from the boxes he'd brought, was a good one.

He'd run it by her, and then listen to her thoughts on the matter before determining a final course.

Hands in the pockets of the dress pants he was still wearing, he solidified his plans as he approached her house.

They might not be personally involved, but they had business to discuss between just the two of them.

The light was on in her craft room.

From outside the back door, he texted her to let her know he was there and wanted to talk.

What's wrong?

Her text came through just as he heard her pull open the back door. As though she'd sent the response verbally while running through the house.

"Nothing's wrong," he said the second her worried face appeared, shadowed beneath the light from the back porch. "I just wanted to talk."

She didn't deny they needed conversation.

He took that as a good sign.

She didn't invite him in, either, suggesting instead that they take a walk. In jean shorts, a tank and cowboy boots, she looked ready to tackle the desert at night. He was up for whatever she needed as long as she was talking to him.

"I had no idea my mother texted you after we broke up," he said, the first thing that came to mind. Not at all what he'd come to converse about.

She shrugged. Said nothing.

They weren't going to be talking about it.

"I also didn't think about the fact that you cared about her, too. Not back then."

Another shrug.

He'd never reached out to anyone in her family. Nor had they attempted to contact him. He figured it wouldn't have been a caring contact as his mother's had been to her.

Getting nowhere with the things clamoring around inside him, feeling like he never would until they could have a real talk, like they used to during college, Jordon told her about the list's arrival. Put his suggestions for their use of it on the table. Heard her praise for the idea, followed immediately by her acceptance of it.

Didn't feel any better.

"I miss you," he said then, under cover of the night, interrupted with bold bright security lights all along the path they were on, winding through parts of the dude ranch.

He heard her intake of breath, sensed that she was about to bolt, and said, "I know there is no us to be had, Mia, but we need to find something in the ashes of what we were that can live in who we are."

So now he was a poet. Or a sap.

"I know."

His chin dropped, his mouth open, as he looked over at her.

"It keeps popping up, doesn't it?"

What did? If she could just answer that question

for him, maybe he'd be better able to grasp what they were going to be. Not having any answers, he nodded.

"Who we used to be, how well we knew each other. Our habits."

Like the toast he'd tried to make the night in the suite. "Yes."

"I used to feel like I could tell you anything," she said then.

Had he felt the same? He wasn't sure he'd ever felt that free. With anyone.

And yet... "Maybe that's what we need to salvage," he said. "The part we need to bring from the past into the future."

Clarity felt within his grasp.

Could it be that simple?

"Our way going forward is to be people who can tell each other anything?" she asked, and he couldn't tell if she thought that was a good idea or a terrible one.

And suddenly he was scrambling again. What did she need him to say to make her feel okay?

Then quiet came over him. Inside his mind. He could still hear the crickets. Sounds of voices from the cabins in the distance. But inside, everything stopped.

That's what he'd done. He'd said what he'd thought she'd wanted him to say so that he could make her happy.

He'd also believed that once they graduated and

real life had to start, she'd see the sense in leaving Shelter Valley, just as her brother and sister had.

Just as her brother had told him he expected her to do.

And Lincoln wasn't the case at hand at the moment.

His honesty was. He'd made the vow. There was nothing he could say that could possibly make Mia Jones happy except the truth.

Even that might not do it. But speaking it was his only chance.

Something else was abundantly clear. "Your happiness matters to me, Mia. Not just because I'm sorry for the past, for hurting you, for leading you on—I know it's pretty impossible to believe but I never meant to do that—lead you on. I really thought you'd realize that leaving Shelter Valley was the obvious choice for our future…"

She'd slowed her step. To turn around?

He didn't blame her. They'd said they were done with that part of the past.

"I would like it if our way going forward would be to be able to speak with each other about anything," he said then. "It's becoming clear to me that it's the only way we're going to make this work. We can't just keep burying things, pretending they aren't there, walking away, because if we don't deal with them as they arise, they'll fester."

He slid his hands into his pockets. Breathing evenly. They had children. They had to find a way to make it work.

"Us walking on eggshells all the time, being afraid to speak for fear of saying the wrong thing, or hurting each other, or making each other angry... that's not going to work for long." He kept talking.

She was keeping pace with him.

"And we've made the commitment now. We're in this forever."

That was it. All he had. Right there in the open.

When she chuckled, he stopped walking. What the hell...

"Talk about ashes from the past, Jordon. This is one of the things that I missed when you were gone."

"Walking in the desert?"

"No, you being able to cut through the crap to get to the point. To bring it to light so that we could solve it."

Right up until that last night. Because he'd landed in a quagmire of four years of his own crap and the only way out he'd seen was to go alone.

"So...we're good?" he asked, just to be sure.

"We're good," she told him, nudging her shoulder against his.

It wasn't a hug. Or anything close to a kiss.

But Jordon felt as though he'd just had the best first date ever. Even better than the first time he'd taken Mia out.

Because this one was ending with them joined together forever.

Chapter Twenty

The next days were a whirlwind for Mia. Reconnecting with Layla was far better than she'd have imagined it could be. They didn't discuss Jordon. And other than that, they took up right where they'd left off. The bond between them…she hadn't imagined it.

Layla hadn't just been motherly to her because she was Jordon's fiancée. But because she'd truly cared for Mia.

It was…nice…knowing that.

Better than nice.

And Layla in the picture, nannying for the girls during their months in New York, made the future seem a whole lot more doable for Mia. Not because she didn't trust Jordon to be a great father, but because she knew Layla would keep her posted, include her, in the little things that mattered to a mother.

Having Layla there, a go-between for Mia and Jordon when they got back to living across the country in their regular daily lives, set Mia's mind at ease. She finally let herself start to believe that they were going to make it work in a way that made everyone happy.

Layla stayed at the cabin that first night, with Jordon sleeping on the couch. She'd wanted to be present when the girls woke up. And her presence allowed Mia to get up at her normal time and get some work done before she joined the girls and Layla for breakfast.

As they moved to the larger cabin, that first day became their routine. Mia still had her time alone with the girls. Layla would cook or borrow Mia's car and go into Phoenix to see friends. And they'd meet up in the afternoon for swimming before dinner.

She didn't see Jordon as much and told herself that that was good, too. Life lost a little spark, but because the spark had come with the danger of her being burned, she was able to relax and enjoy every second she had with Ruby and Violet.

And every moment became precious, too, and maybe a little fraught with dread, as the end of the month drew closer and she knew that Jordon would be taking the girls back to New York. He'd said he'd fly to New York sometime that next week, leaving

Layla with Mia and the girls, and then fly out west
again to take them home.

Home.

New York would be her daughters' home. Not hers.

And her home wouldn't be theirs.

Every time the thought sent panic through her,
she reminded herself that until the beginning of that
month, she hadn't even known she had children.

And that, having no legal rights to them, she was
blessed to be so included in their lives.

Her mind got it fully.

Her heart…cried a bit.

Even while it rejoiced.

She'd called her brother and sister, a video call the
first full day that Layla was there, to tell them that
the twins were hers, and after they'd calmed down
and she firmly assured them that she was happier
than she'd ever been, they were excited to meet their
nieces. By Thursday, they'd made plans to visit that
weekend, and even that had gone well.

Lincoln and Jordon didn't say much to each other,
which was fine with Mia. But on that Saturday evening, they all met at the dude ranch's convention
cabin—a place where employers could hold functions with their employees during bonding weeks,
or families could have reunions while staying at the
cabins—and had a loud and lively dinner together.
Ruby and Violet were the youngest by several years
but found their places in the family as though they'd
been born there.

Her ten-year-old nephew had taken Ruby and Violet under his wing, showing them how to catch a ball, and they'd both adored him. Running after him everywhere he went. Her nieces, aged eight and nine, had tried to baby the girls and ended up playing house with them. Ruby and Violet were besotted, so played along well at being the "kids" and taking orders from the "parents" until they were done and ran off to play ball and then to collect pretty rocks.

Layla had met both Lincoln and Sara and Lincoln's spouse during holiday events at the ranch when Mia and Jordon were in college and, by appearances at least, seemed to enjoy reconnecting. Sara's husband, Randy, was a genuinely nice guy, a stay-at-home dad, who got along with, and watched over, everyone.

Greg Richards, the sheriff of Shelter Valley, stopped by in time for dessert, almost as though he'd known exactly when to show up—as Mia was certain he had. He brought his wife, Beth, with him, and she was as gracious and lovely as always. Her son, Ryan, had been two when she'd shown up in town with no memory of who she was or how she got there, and the sheriff had fallen hook, line and sinker. Mia had been ten or eleven at the time. Ryan had just graduated from Montford with a degree in law enforcement. The Richards had two biological kids of their own, too, both in high school.

And when she'd introduced Ruby and Violet, while they'd both shown surprise, she could tell they'd already known the twins were her biological children. And she had her confirmation as to who had tipped her brother off to the twins' arrival at the ranch two weeks before. It had been Greg, just as she'd thought.

Because of Greg's loyalty to Lincoln, Mia had been a little unsure of the sheriff's reaction to Jordon being among them, but, true to Shelter Valley's ways, Greg welcomed Jordon back to the fold. It's what Shelter Valley people did.

They gave second chances.

Which was why, after everyone had retired to their own places for the night, and Mia said goodnight to the girls, intending to stop by and see Brilliant before heading up to her big house alone, she'd accepted Jordon's offer to walk up with her.

In the two weeks he'd been back in her life, he'd done everything he could to make things right with her. He'd given her her children. Was sharing them with her permanently.

It was time she was good to him, too. Not just decent. Polite. But good.

While their personal past was gone forever, they could find a new "them." He'd said as much the previous week, on their walk, and while she'd agreed with him, she hadn't been able to commit to any kind of personal interaction between them that didn't directly involve the girls.

She'd been denying him his second chance.

But as they walked up the dirt road from the cabins to her place, she struggled for words. How did you ask your ex, the probable love of your life, to be your friend?

It was a question she'd take to Brilliant.

"You want to meet someone?" she asked, kind of regretting the question as soon as she'd uttered it. But somehow knowing that introducing him to the friend who'd saved her after Jordon had left was the right bridge from past to present.

"Here?" he asked, looking far too good in the shorts and polo shirt he'd had on all day. With everyone else around, she'd been able to avoid any direct eye contact with his muscled chest and thighs and butt.

"Of course, here," she told him. Wondering if the trepidation she felt was getting through to him somehow.

Like she was making too much of him meeting her horse.

The girls had seen Brilliant. Had seen Mia tending to the horse, as she did others during the day. They didn't know she was hers.

Jordon didn't accept her request. But he kept pace with her as she turned off from the road and segued over to the biggest barn, and then, flipping on the back wall lights only, headed toward Brilliant's stall in the back corner.

Opening the door of the stall, she whispered a few words of greeting, and then, keeping her voice soft, nestled up to the horse's head as Brilliant stood, flapped her tail back and forth and reached for Mia with her nose.

"This is Brilliant," Mia said, turning toward Jordon, who'd stepped just inside the stall. As if on cue, the mare rested her head on Mia's shoulder.

As though the horse knew who Jordon was. And was claiming ownership of the heart Jordon broke.

Jordon didn't step forward. Or move back, either. He stood there, nodded at the horse. And waited.

He knew something was coming. She could tell by the set of his shoulders. His jaw.

She liked that, knowing him well enough to figure out where he was at just by looking at him. And kind of hated knowing, too. It spoke of a closeness she no longer wanted with him.

Her mind didn't want.

The heart…it had been given to him long ago and apparently there were no take backs.

Grabbing a brush off the shelf, she started soft, sure strokes along Brilliant's lower neck. The horse's coat didn't need attention. Brilliant just loved the touching.

And Mia needed to touch.

"After you left…I was frozen inside. Couldn't find anything to be excited about. Nothing to look forward to. That part of me…it was just gone."

She didn't look at him. "My father tried to get me interested in things. Talking my sister into taking me to stay with her on the beach in San Diego for a few days. All I wanted was to get back to Shelter Valley."

That part wouldn't surprise him.

"But even being home…I couldn't find anything I wanted. Not to eat. Not to do. I worked. Damned hard. I had a plan.

"I just didn't care."

The silence behind her was acute. For all she knew, Jordon had quietly walked out on her. She didn't check.

If he didn't have what it took to get them to a different place, then he didn't. She couldn't blame him.

Any more than she could blame herself for who she was.

"My dad was failing…"

He'd known that. Had actually used that in his plea to get her to leave, saying that the only reason her father was still trying to keep the ranch going was because of her. That if she'd go, she'd let him off the hook and he could sell the ranch and use the profits to move into a really nice independent living place and take it easy.

He hadn't known her dad as well as she'd thought he had.

"He knew he wasn't going to be around forever. So one day he went out with his truck and came back with a horse trailer. And one horse."

With the brush in one hand, she smoothed her other lovingly against Brilliant's neck.

"Brilliant," she said. And then, "This girl saved my life."

She turned then, half expecting Jordon to be gone.

Felt a flare of intensity when she saw him still standing there, right where she'd last seen him.

His gaze moving from the horse to her. Back and forth.

"If you're trying to tell me that this is the life you need, Mia, you don't have to," he said.

She shook her head. "I'm in the process of getting to what I wanted to tell you." She spoke directly to him. Then turned back to Brilliant for a second before leaving the horse's side, returning the brush to where it belonged and leaning her shoulder against the stall, facing Jordon.

"I didn't love Shelter Valley more than I loved you." That's what he deserved to know. Her truth where they were concerned.

She couldn't be anything to him without being honest.

"I couldn't leave, not without hating myself. It wasn't about the town, Jordon, the place."

His gaze broke from hers, but came back almost immediately, a bit more shadowed than it had been, and she added, "I love it here more than anywhere else on earth. I feel…right…here. Like I belong. But it was the people I couldn't leave. My father, mostly, that I couldn't leave."

Jordon's arms crossed, and she heard how that sounded.

"Not because I loved him more or was too much a baby to leave my parent. But because he'd given my brother and sister and me his whole life, Jordon. Sara and Lincoln had both left him. They could because I was still home. But who'd be there for him if I left?

"Moving him off the ranch would have killed him. Not that it would have come to that. He'd have refused to leave. I never understood how you missed that point. He'd have died alone with the house falling apart around him. While I was, what—off in New York having sex and babies and what else, Jordon? What life was there for me? You'd be off at your dinners and business parties and functions and I'd be...what? Sitting there feeling like scum because I was thinking of myself and what I wanted and letting my father slowly die alone? Because I'd have nothing else there. You didn't figure a place for my daily life, in your plans."

And...there was more.

"The ranch was my father's legacy," she said then. "And mine, too. I needed to use my college degree to make a living out of it, just like you needed to use yours on Wall Street."

Telling him about Brilliant, having him meet her mare...it was going someplace. Jordon needed to know how much she'd loved him.

He wasn't saying anything.

His chin was working though. She could only guess what he'd heard in the words she'd said.

"I listened to you back then," he finally spoke, his voice as soft as hers had been. "I just thought I had a clearer picture of how things would work out best."

There was no fight in him. No defensiveness.

Which surprised her. And knocked her heart around some, too.

"I didn't factor in your father, or my mother, either. I thought about us. Heading out into the world to start our lives together."

"To start your life…" she had to point out. He'd left no room for her life. Not anywhere in his plans.

"And if we'd stayed here…it would have been your life," he answered back.

He was right. To a point. She'd envisioned him in Phoenix, working just as he had the past couple of weeks. She'd made room for his life.

But didn't say so. Because the room she'd made— it hadn't been the life he'd wanted.

"So, we were right to split up," she said then. Finding some kind of peace in the moment. There was sadness, too.

But if it got them to the future—to a friendship that could be comfortable while they raised their daughters together, albeit apart, too—then a little sadness was a small price to pay.

Jordon didn't approach the horse. After an evening with Mia's family, he wasn't feeling all that fond of himself and had a feeling the horse would know it.

It clearly knew her.

"You didn't beg me to stay."

The words were juvenile. Probably a stupid thing to say.

First, "You loved Shelter Valley more than you

loved me." And now that? Where was this stuff coming from?

"How could I beg you to give up everything you wanted?"

"I wanted you."

"Just not as much as you wanted New York."

There was no recrimination. Just a search for truth that would put the past to rest. That's what they needed.

"New York was my future in terms of having money to provide. To live the type of life I wanted my family to be able to live. A home that was big enough for sleepovers, and not in constant need of repair. Money in the bank to pay bills and buy groceries without having to worry, every single month, if there'd be enough. And on the months that there wasn't, settling for eating from a big pot of homemade tomato soup until the next paycheck."

He regretted the words as soon as he said them. Had never, in his life, said them before.

"I had no idea... I knew your house was small, but I never thought anything of it. It had been just the two of you. And yeah, it had needed some work, but so had the farm. A ton of it. I'd thought we were alike in that way. That coming from beat-up homes was part of what drew us together. Something we had in common. But I never had to worry about a full kitchen. Or paying bills. It was more that my father couldn't keep up with the farm duties. Acreage was going without being planted. The tractor was failing and it was a vicious cycle, but..."

They could always sell the farm. Which would have made them, if not rich, at least comfortable. Which was why it had made perfect sense to Jordon that they do so. He was a finance man. A guy who looked at assets and knew how best to turn them into security and more assets.

Just as his mother had made the tomatoes she grew into sustenance to keep them alive until there was money to buy groceries.

"I never told anyone about how hard it was," he said then. "Mom and I never talked about it, either. We just dealt with it."

He hadn't said anything because he'd been ashamed.

And wasn't fond of that point.

Nor did he share it.

"I'll bet she was thrilled when you bought her the condo on the river," she said, letting him know that his mother had done as he'd suspected, given Mia a rundown on her life.

"She's never said one way or the other. Truth be told, I don't think it mattered to her all that much. She just wanted to be close to me."

That had been another eye-opener. And yet, none of it changed much.

He was who he was. He had to provide for the future.

And his skill set, his drive, his passion, his talent, was trading up, making more out of less.

Mia straightened. Said good-night to her horse and led them quietly out of the barn and into the night.

Apparently, they were done.

He wasn't ready but was relieved just the same.

Chapter Twenty-One

Mia wasn't surprised when Jordon texted on Monday to say he'd booked a flight to New York leaving Tuesday morning. He hoped to be back by the weekend, and then fly with Layla and the kids back to the East Coast that Sunday. It made sense, he said, to have his mother on the trip with them.

She responded with supportive remarks and fought the instinct to go hug her girls to her and never let go. Or hide them someplace just until the threat of their leaving passed.

The threat wasn't going to pass.

And even if she had full custody of the girls and could force the situation to be what she wanted, she'd still send them to spend good portions of time with their father in New York.

It was an odd situation, but the girls needed both of them. And they were going to make it work.

Yes, it would probably be best for Ruby and Violet if she and Jordon could just be a couple again, get married and live happily ever after. In one place.

But she and Jordon were too different. One or the other of them would have to completely give up their sense of self in order for them to live in one place, which would lead to unhappiness, at the very least. And an unhappy home wouldn't be good for the twins. Or worst case, it would lead to another breakup between them and that would most definitely be bad for their daughters because it would preclude the friendship they were forging.

It was all happening for the best.

And they *were* going to make it work.

On and off that day, she played the litany over in her mind. Watching the girls swimming in the pool, putting their whole heads underwater. Leading them around the stable on the ranch's smallest, gentlest horses. She made a silent promise to her sweet little ones that she and Jordon would not let them down.

Their lives wouldn't be cookie-cutter perfect. But they'd be well loved. And well-rounded, too. Hopefully gaining confidence in themselves and their ability to make their own ways in the world as they flew back and forth across the country and grew up with two different lifestyles.

Some would judge. Some would find them incredibly lucky with all the opportunities they'd be given.

It was harder to send them off for bath and story time Monday night, knowing that their time with her had an end date and that it would be months, perhaps many of them, before she got to read to them at night again.

Still, when Jordon got home and stopped at the house to pick up the girls on his way to the cabin where Layla was making their dinner, she sent them off with a wave and smile.

Reminding herself that a couple of weeks ago, she'd not only have been dining without them, but she hadn't even known she had children, let alone that she was going to get to be a mother to them.

Reminding herself not to be selfish. No one got to have it all. That would leave someone else with nothing.

A quote she'd heard along the way. Accepted. But didn't really like.

To her way of thinking, everyone should have everything. She looked at life in abundance, not scarcity.

She needed to get into town. The Shelter Valley women's group—a tradition started by the town's mayor when Mia was just a kid—was having dinner on campus that night. She'd never actually attended the unofficial night out designed to accommodate any women in town who wanted to give or take some sisterly uplifting, but she'd been invited many times. By several people, including the mayor herself, Becca Parsons.

That night, Mia went. And was shocked when she walked into the catered event and was immediately swamped by women she'd known her whole life. All clamoring over to her. To congratulate her. Hug her. Offer to babysit. Or to commiserate during the long months the girls weren't with her. There were questions in the eyes of many.

None were asked.

And as tears filled her eyes, Mia knew she'd waited too long to avail herself of the bounty her life had to offer her—and others. Maybe she'd hadn't actually opened back up her heart as much as she'd thought she had.

But she would.

And keep it open, too.

Jordon might have broken her heart, but she'd been the one who'd failed to let it fully heal. She'd blamed him when the fault hadn't really been his. Other than leading her to believe that he was okay with a life in Shelter Valley. But even that, he hadn't been overtly lying. He'd been a kid believing that he saw a light she'd see eventually. He'd been keeping the light burning for both of them, to his way of thinking.

And she'd let his actions blow her light out.

Jordon had to talk to Mia. He couldn't take the leap—introduce his New York life to the imminent advent of his daughters into his world—without being fully honest with Mia.

They had to know, once and for all, that they could follow through on their new life plans. He was afraid that if he texted her, she'd simply tell him she was working, busy, whatever. Or, because the girls were at his cabin asleep, not with her, she'd simply fail to respond at all.

Ditto a phone call.

As soon as his mother settled down with the book she was reading, he placed the baby monitor beside her and told her he was going for a walk.

The long look she gave him, the softening in her gaze, reached out to him. But she said nothing. Just nodded.

Mia's office light wasn't on. Only a light over the kitchen sink was visible.

Jordon checked out the garage, looking in the window to see her car not there.

And sat down on her back porch step to wait for her. Not even sorry for what he was doing.

She didn't want him figuring out what was best all on his own, then she was going to have to talk to him.

He saw her headlights first, coming straight up the drive instead of turning to go up to the cabins. Didn't move from his position on the steps as she turned, and then moved on into the garage door that had just risen on its own.

Still in the dress pants, shirt, loosened tie and shoes he'd worn to work, and to another gathering that afternoon, he left his elbows where they were, resting on his knees, and waited.

Watched her leave the garage and head his way. He didn't know if she'd seen him. Didn't much care.

She'd know he was there soon enough.

He didn't stand to greet her. They were on her property. He wasn't the greeter.

Nor did he want a standoff.

He wasn't there to fight.

She looked different. She was wearing a black short-sleeved dress that fell halfway down her thighs, leaving plenty exposed to him, and black flip-flops with lots of silver bling. He focused on the bling. Cowgirl bling, he told himself. Like the belt buckle he'd seen her wear when she'd ridden horses in college.

Her hair, wild as always, seemed to purposefully tease him as she came closer.

She'd seen him. She couldn't not. She was staring right at him.

She didn't slow down. Just came right up and took a seat on the long step beside him. Leaving a good foot between them.

Was way too much space. And not nearly enough.

She said nothing.

He'd called the meeting. She was apparently content to wait for him to begin. Not even questioning his right to have done so in the first place.

Like they were beyond that.

He hoped so.

"My response to the court on your behalf has been filed," he started in. "I explained that the entire idea

to donate the material to make embryos had been
yours and stated that the Robinsons had no way to
get in touch with you because you chose to donate
anonymously so that Madeline never had another
woman in mind as she was growing her babies. So
that she felt they were fully hers."

It was the reason she'd given him, and while he
hadn't quite grasped the magnitude of what she'd
been saying, he'd never forgotten it, either.

Mia sat quietly, her arms around her knees.

"Lastly, I asked the court to grant your wish for
visitation rights and substantiated the request with
examples from the past couple of weeks that exem-
plify why the girls need you in their lives."

She hadn't dropped her arms. If anything, she was
hugging her legs more tightly. But she'd turned her
head to look at him, her expression made stark by
the shadows of night blending with moonlight and
security lights in the distance.

He could almost feel the deep breath she took, and
when her jaw moved, to speak, he figured, he said,
"There's more."

He couldn't be sidetracked by anything that might
come out of her mouth.

And chances were, no matter what she said, he'd
be sidetracked.

Mia had a way of doing that to him. Taking him
on her verbal journeys and tying him up in ways that
were detrimental to the platonic friendship they were
going to have for the rest of their lives.

And to get there…

To stay there…

"I told you that partially so that you understand that I'm one hundred percent committed to making this work," he said. "Because the other thing I have to tell you might make you doubt me."

Oh no. Hadn't meant to say that. Couldn't rewind. Nothing to do but go forward.

"I love you."

Stark. Ungarnished.

Truth.

Mia's skin chilled as her body heated up.

What in the hell was he doing?

Expecting her to do?

Wanting from her?

If he…

He'd just pretty much put the seal on her certainty of getting legal rights to the girls. According to her attorney, Jordon's response would carry the only real weight against granting her request, if he'd chosen to fight it. He couldn't take back his support. Not with his response officially filed. Not without cause and she'd give him none.

At some point within the next few months, the court would rule and chances were almost certain she'd have legal rights.

He was in it for the long haul.

And…

"You aren't saying anything."

"I have no idea why you just said that." And couldn't deal with what the words meant. Figure out what he'd wanted them to mean.

How she was supposed to take them.

"I failed to communicate with total and open honesty in the past. I am doing everything I can to make certain that I don't repeat the mistake going forward."

"And, so what, you give me the response to my filing and then confuse the issue?"

"It's not meant to confuse, Mia. But to educate."

"What do you want me to do?"

"Nothing."

Like that was going to happen. He might not know what she was going to do, but no way she could hear something like that and just pretend it hadn't happened.

"You love me like a friend?" she asked. "Like a copartner in the biggest venture of our lives?"

"I'm in love with you, Mia." His tone was kind. Soft. And unmistakably certain. "I never stopped loving you."

So…did he want to try again?

The idea sent shock waves through her. Not all bad ones.

Some very not bad ones.

There were some not good ones, too.

But…did he want to try again?

Did she?

"I don't… I can't… I…"

"This doesn't change anything."

His words fell into the cacophony rumbling around inside her mind. Making no sense.

"It changes everything." She practically cried the words.

"No." He met her panicked gaze, his look clear. Calm. "It doesn't."

"But..."

He reached out a hand, ran his fingers through her hair and then palmed her cheek. Leaning over, he kissed her.

Her lips answered his. Naturally. Automatically. Without permission. But she didn't pull back.

He did.

"I'm sorry," he said. And then followed with, "I didn't intend that part."

She needed to get in the house. To take a shower and wash off her wanting him. To cry and pretend the water on her face was from above. Not inside.

"What did you intend?" Her voice shook, ending on a louder note.

His gaze still didn't break with hers. He was oddly sure about whatever it was he was doing to her.

And she was more off-kilter than she'd ever been.

"To start out with everything on the table so that we both know what's here. So there aren't any surprises down the road."

Oh. So, he really meant he wanted nothing more?

"You think you can tell me that and we just go on with our plan as agreed upon?"

"I think we have no other choice but to go on as agreed," he said then, his elbows back on his knees, hands clasped.

Hands that had felt so right, so wonderful, touching her again.

"We've been over it all," he continued. "Your life is here. Mine is in New York. What you do, what you love to do, it's here. On this ranch. In this town. And my life is in New York. It's as you said. I didn't think about what you'd actually do, for a living, to complete you, or even to occupy yourself on a daily basis, in New York. I just saw how much we loved each other and I couldn't imagine my life without you."

She'd been right. Understanding helped ease past weights.

But she felt zero vindication. She didn't need Jordon to be wrong. To have wronged her. She needed them to be able to be happy. Both of them.

"And if we try, and it doesn't work, the girls suffer," she said then.

He nodded.

Had obviously already laid the matter to rest. She wasn't there yet.

He'd had a head start on her.

"You ever consider a long-distance relationship? Traveling back and forth?" She could live three weeks on the ranch. Or even two. And the other two in the city. And he could leave the city for two weeks. He'd just proven so...

"With kids in school? How would that work?"

They could be homeschooled. But she got his point. Because their future together was all about raising happy, healthy daughters. Those girls needed stability. Friends. Dance or art or swimming classes. An opportunity to participate in sports. One place to call home.

And another to call summers on the ranch.

"The truth is, you're at your best here, Mia. And I'm at my best in New York."

And asking either of them to be anything but their best wasn't love.

She nodded. Leaned over and kissed him.

Once. Softly.

"I love you, too," she said, feeling the tears pressing at her.

And got up and went inside.

Chapter Twenty-Two

Landing in New York felt...odd. Incomplete. Glad to be on familiar soil at least, home soil, Jordon collected the car he'd left in long-term parking. Drove to the garage a mile from his apartment building. Grabbed his suitcase, his briefcase, and caught a cab home from the closest garage to his building.

He did what he always did when returning from a trip.

Routine.

And was somehow off his mark. Hitting his shin with his suitcase as he pulled it off the conveyor in baggage claim. Catching a finger in the handle of his briefcase when he climbed into the cab.

Hitting the elevator door in his building with his thigh as he entered.

As soon as word had hit the day before that he was going to be in Tuesday evening, invitations had started hitting his text and email inboxes.

He'd accepted three of them. Had lost time to make up for and was going to be gone again over the weekend.

Once he showered, had a fresh shave and was wearing evening clothes, he'd be back in his groove.

But first, he phoned Layla. To let her know he'd made it safely, for some unknown reason. He hadn't called his mother after a trip specifically just to check in since…well, ever?

And he talked to Ruby and Violet together on a video call.

"Jordon Daddy?" Violet screwed up her face when she first saw him on the screen. "When are you coming home?"

"Are you coming home in thirty?" Ruby asked then. "I can count to thirty, 'member?"

"Yeah, me too!" Violet said, pushing her face a little closer. Not pushing her sister out of the way, but clearly making herself front and center.

"And we got pichers of riding. Mama Mia taked them," Violet said.

He'd seen them. The second he'd turned on his phone when they'd landed on the runway. Mia had sent them. He'd texted back a heart emoji.

And then, in the spirit of full communication, had told her that he was still in the plane, but that they'd landed.

She'd responded with a thumbs-up.

"I can't wait for you to show me your pictures," he told both girls. He asked what they'd had for lunch. If they'd been swimming, and what book they wanted Gran to read to them before bed. Listened to their sweet lispy answers. Watching the clock, taking every spare minute he could, and then told them that he loved them and to sleep well.

"When are you coming home, Jordon Daddy?" Violet asked again then.

"In four sleeps," he replied. "Which is why you need to go get one of them done."

"Okay!" Violet said. "Come on, Ruby, let's go to sleep and then Jordon Daddy will be back!"

Didn't seem to matter that it was only three in the afternoon their time.

Ruby, who'd obviously been holding the phone, dropped it, leaving Jordon to stare at something light beige. Up real close.

Until his mother picked up the cell, and laughingly told him goodbye.

It was nice. Being a part of something of his own.

Feeling better, Jordon left for an evening of energized work in the name of socialization.

And wished he had Mia at his side when he went out to hail a cab.

Right up until he got to his first stop—a gathering with drinks and hors d'oeuvres and some of Wall Street's top investors—and saw all of the makeup, jewels and expensive dresses in the crowded room and knew that it would all choke Mia to death.

The week flew by in a blink. Layla, who was thriving back in the blue skies, sunshine and heat of the desert, had reconnected with friends in Phoenix and opted to spend the rest of the days Jordon was gone, in the city, spending time with Gloria and a couple of their mutual friends, before heading back to New York.

Which had left Mia three days and three nights with her girls all to herself. Herself, plus Mariah Macy's Mom and half a dozen others on the ranch as well. But for meals, bath time, story time and bed-time, they were all hers.

She soaked up every moment.

Took so many pictures and videos she had to get a bigger memory card for her phone.

And knew a happiness she'd never imagined.

Jordon was in touch every day. Several times a day. Just communicating, he called it. Asking her opinion on bed styles, dresser drawer pulls, color schemes and shower curtain design. They discussed the girls in detail.

They never asked after each other.

And neither even got close to mentioning their last in-person conversation. It was as though it had never happened.

Except that Mia couldn't get it out of her head.

They'd loved each other ten years before, just as

she'd thought. It hadn't been a lie. Her heart had been true.

And so had his been.

It was their lives, their persons, that weren't suited. Not their hearts.

Didn't matter.

Heart and person went together. You didn't get one without the other.

And yet, knowing…understanding…what had happened…knowing what parts of her relationship with Jordon had been real—gave life a whole new dimension.

Jordon called at bedtime each night, talking to the girls and counting down sleeps until he was back.

She knew he'd just come in, or, on the second night, was still out but had stepped into a quiet alcove to call—but she didn't ask him where he was, what he was doing or who he was with.

And he didn't say.

Part of her wanted to know, in a kick herself in the teeth way. But mostly, she trusted that Jordon was doing what he needed to do and he'd do so while protecting those he cared about.

And that was new to her older self. Nice.

Introduced another dimension to the future they planned. One that sat well with her.

All was well right up until Jordon caught a flight out on Friday, after the bell rang, rather than waiting until Saturday as originally planned.

He'd wanted to have all day Saturday at the ranch

with the girls, to talk to them, prepare, spend time with Mia and with them so they understood that they were a happy family together even though they weren't going to live together all the time, before leaving on Sunday.

Once she'd heard about it, she fully understood, and embraced his thinking.

Problem was, since Layla left, she'd rented out his cabin through Friday night—to be available again before his Saturday arrival, and he didn't let her know his change of plans before he arrived. Which meant that he showed up in Shelter Valley without a place to stay. He'd planned, apparently, to go to the cabin, have a little time to himself to unwind, and surprise the girls first thing in the morning.

With a text to Mia to inform her before he actually showed up at the house.

Instead, she got a text just after she'd put the girls to bed, letting her know that there were people in his cabin.

As though they'd just happened to have a key or had broken in, and were openly on the deck having after-dinner drinks with family members from the next cabin?

Come up to the house, she texted back. She couldn't have him parked down at the dude ranch, glaring at her guests.

And didn't want to tell him over text that she'd rented out the place she'd told him he could use as long as he was in town.

Baby monitor in hand, she waited for him outside. On the back step, since he'd chosen that destination the week before.

Though darkness had fallen, she could see clouds in the sky, illuminated by the moon obscured behind them. The pinkish heat lightning transformed the desert sky into a glorious light show. Had she been alone, she'd have brought out her equipment and filmed a few shots to use as background for an upcoming boho wall hanging that had the same colors.

As it was, she absorbed the beauty, the electricity, the potential for danger, as she stood there and watched as the father of her children exited his vehicle—all dressed up in New York style as usual—and headed toward her.

The lightning burst, sending shards of light all over his tall, lean body, highlighting the chest behind buttoned-down cotton.

He could cover that chest, but nothing hid the magnetism.

And she couldn't hide her desire for him from herself any longer, either. They'd admitted they still loved each other.

He'd been the only man to spark both her body and her heart full force. Opening the one had set the other free, as well. She'd been fighting herself on the matter all week.

When she'd just been attracted to him, as had been the case since he'd walked back into her life—

muscle memory, she'd assumed—she could keep things under control.

But knowing he still loved her...

His confession had unleashed a power that could hurt them if they didn't deal with it.

But not then.

That was a conversation to have with him sometime when he was in New York. Safely across the country and firmly out of reach.

They'd find a solution for animalism just as they had every other challenge that had come at them over the past weeks.

He'd always liked her natural style. Maybe she'd start wearing fashionable clothes, let her hair grow out and get professional instruction for globbing up her face with makeup.

Once he no longer found her attractive, her own desire would die.

"You rented out my cabin." He said the words as he approached.

"Just until tomorrow morning," she told him. "It would have been cleaned and ready before you got back."

His lower lip jutting, he gave a half shrug. Nodded.

Had to be tired. He'd worked all day, at a job that took a lot of energy. Then he'd dealt with busy airports, flown across the country, rented a vehicle and had driven an hour over a dark desert highway.

"You can stay here." The words spilled out. But

she didn't regret them. "I changed the sheets on the bed Layla used."

When he didn't respond, she said, "I thought you knew your mom went to the city for a few days. She wanted to spend some time with her friends before leaving on Sunday. And…I think, though she didn't say…she wanted to give me some time alone with the girls."

"She told me."

"There's a family reunion," she told him. "A brother and his wife who hadn't thought they could make it suddenly could. Your cabin was sitting there empty."

"I understand."

He was standing all right. Right in front of her. With the sky exploding above him.

"Come inside, Jordon."

He shook his head. "I'll drive back to the city. Get a room there."

His suggestion was better for their lifetime plan. Safer. She needed to shut up and let him go.

She didn't want him driving another hour on dark roads. Not after the day he'd had.

"The girls would be super excited to see you here when they wake up in the morning."

Hands in his pockets, he pinned her with a stare she didn't expect. "And how excited would you be to see me in your room tonight?"

Mouth open, she couldn't look away. The moon. The lightning. Him. They were sucking her in. She was already wet.

Honesty. That was their game plan.

"I'd be super excited," she said then. "But..."

He nodded. "I know."

Did that mean he was going back to Phoenix?

Disappointment crashed through her.

"Maybe it would be okay," she said softly, taking a step closer to him. "We're already sharing two little people. We could share a bed now and then, too. It's not like we haven't done it before."

"You need commitment."

She shook her head, the sky seemingly inside her now, lighting her on fire. "I believe what I said I need is love."

His gaze sharpened. It was like he could see straight inside her to her deepest thoughts.

"It's not like it could become something more with us living across the country from each other." His body didn't touch her. His words caressed her nipples, hardening them.

"Just something that happens now and then, as long as neither of us is in a relationship and we both want it." She was ready to jump him, as she had the night he'd asked her to marry him.

Taking a deep breath, Jordon maintained the distance between them. "You're sure?"

"I'm sure that occasional sex with you would be one hell of a lot better than being celibate." Beyond that, she didn't know.

Except... "Don't worry, Jordon, I won't build it into more than it is. I know you're taking the girls and going home. I support that choice. Just as you support them living here with me during the summer months." She didn't love the setup because it meant she missed much of her daughters' growing up. Had no idea how she was going to cope when they drove off the ranch on Sunday. But she understood that it was the best option for all of them going forward.

"It's not you I'm worried about." She thought she heard the words. He'd uttered them beneath his breath. She couldn't be sure…

Before she could respond his lips were on hers. Completely differently than they had been the week before. It was a lovers' kiss.

Familiar. Hungry lips moving on hers in a way that told her exactly what was coming.

And she kissed him back.

More ready than she'd ever been.

Chapter Twenty-Three

He savored her. The taste of every inch of her body. The look of every expression on her face. The sound of every moan she made. Every cry that tore out of her.

Far more than he needed the minute of release he'd find in her, he needed to lie with Mia again, touch her, connect with her.

Remember every other time he'd ever been there. Her naked body on a bed with his.

The sex had always been phenomenal.

That night in Mia's bed, on top of her, beneath her, beside her, surpassed anything he'd ever known.

They'd slept. And had risen together, heading to different bathrooms to shower quickly before their daughters awoke. Worked together to have pancakes ready for them.

"Jordon Daddy?" Ruby had scrunched up her little nose as he entered their bedroom first when sounds of rustling covers came over the baby monitor.

"Jordon Daddy's home!" Violet had yelled, standing up to run across their mattress to get to him.

His heart fuller than he'd ever known it could be, he'd savored the moments. Even turning to find Mia gone hadn't expunged his joy.

She was giving him his moments.

Just as he'd give her hers.

He and Mia spent the day not touching each other but giving their daughters complete attention. Mia had suggested that they wait until late afternoon to tell the girls about their departure.

And to make it an adventure ahead, not a separation.

Dreading the moment, half expecting the girls to reject him once they knew he was taking them away, he gladly conceded to her reasoning, and when the time came, he sat beside Mia at the pool, with a twin at the foot of each of the adult loungers.

Swimming lessons were done. The dude ranchers had gone for mess—the Saturday night official cowboy supper consisting of camp bread made in a skillet, dried fruit and dried meat, accompanied by commercial cowboy dinners of barbecue ribs, country fried chicken, fancy baked beans, and grilled corn on the cob and biscuits.

He'd have been glad to procrastinate their dreaded family moment a little longer. But knew she was right to give the girls time to process before dinner and bedtime. They'd be leaving right after breakfast to head to Phoenix to catch their eleven-thirty flight, picking Layla up on their way to the airport.

"How would you two like to get up tomorrow and fly on an airplane?" Jordon started the conversation, instilling his voice with excitement. With no idea how the next moments would transpire.

He couldn't look at Mia. But felt her kind support next to him.

"A airpwane?" Ruby asked.

"Like when we went to see Mickey?" Violet jumped from her butt to her knees in one motion, both hands coming together at the slightly distended little belly in her swimsuit.

He hadn't known they'd been to see Mickey Mouse. There'd been nothing about it in the reports.

"Yes," he said slowly. "Like that. We'll be on an airplane."

Ruby hopped to her knees, too. "We're going to see Mickey?"

At a loss, not wanting to disappoint the two precious expectant faces, he said, "Well..."

"You're going someplace even better!" Mia exclaimed. "To a big city called New York where they have the hugest park, and more lights and things even than Phoenix where you lived before. There are carts with treats in them on every corner. And stores just to sell candy. And ice cream and when it snows, you can learn to ice skate."

Something they wouldn't be able to do in the desert.

"Yay!" both girls cried out with glee as they jumped off the loungers and, hands joined, circled around as they had in Mia's kitchen what seemed eons before.

So far so good. He glanced in Mia's direction.

Saw her smile…and something else in her eyes… as she watched the twins.

A rock landed in his gut.

How could he take them from her?

"There's one more thing," Mia said then and the girls stopped circling to look at her. "I can't fly with you right now, because I have to help Mariah Macy's Mom for a little bit, and also help her keep Macy company while you're on your adventures, but I'll come see you, and then, when it's summer again, you're flying right back here!"

She made it sound so…doable.

He noticed that she didn't ask the girls if the plans were okay with them.

The child life specialist had told them not to give the girls a choice when they didn't have one. And conversely to give them as many choices as they could when the girls had the chance to choose for themselves.

While the twins were still standing there, looking at Mia, he jumped in with, "And guess what?" Grabbing their attention before they had a chance to spiral into all the reasons they might not want to go.

"What?" both girls responded at once, looks of anticipation lighting up their nearly identical faces.

"Gran's coming on the airplane with us!"

"Yay!" both girls cried and started dancing in a joined circle again.

The truth would settle at some point in the next twelve hours. He didn't kid himself about that. Those two little girls adored their mother already.

And they were four. Easily adaptable. They were going to love New York and have so much new to distract them that they'd be fine.

He glanced at Mia, almost as though he was looking for reassurance for himself from her calm demeanor.

Thought he saw her top lip trembling a bit as she grinned at the girls' antics.

And Jordon felt another twinge in his gut.

All day long, Mia had been focusing on the future. Soaking up memories. Hugging her girls as often as she could. And thinking about times she'd visit them all in New York.

With the added pleasure of spending the night in Jordon's bed.

Looking toward the following summer when she'd have them for months, not weeks.

And have sex with Jordon during his visits, too.

A month ago, she'd been living alone, with no other choice on the horizon.

In the space of weeks, she'd become a mother of biological twins and reconnected with the best sex she'd ever had.

Had come to terms with herself—her heart and her soul.

And with the past. Laying it to rest.

The future before her held the life she'd built, the life she loved, plus a whole lot more that she hadn't dared dream she'd have.

And so the sadness that tinged her edges as she gave the girls their baths and read them their story, the one about Spot that they loved, was only bittersweet, not heartbreaking.

When Jordon came in just as she was tucking the girls in, holding his phone out and saying that Gran wanted to say good-night, Mia welcomed the interruption.

And the reminder. She wasn't alone anymore. She had a family of her own, albeit an oddly made one. Layla was back in her life again.

All of them—Mia, Jordon and Layla—were determined to make sure that Ruby and Violet, gifts that they were, would grow up happy, healthy and very much loved.

The fact that the twins were funny, precious, adorable and sweet was just icing on the cake.

Layla was right to remind the girls, just before they fell asleep, that she'd be seeing them in the morning. They'd know fresh in their minds that as they left Mia, they'd be heading to Layla.

With Jordon Daddy.

The one who'd brought them all together.

Mia wasn't quite as peaceful when Layla asked to stay on the line to have a word with Mia and Jordon.

Stomach tight, she immediately went to the worst-case scenario. Layla wasn't going to be a part of their plan. She was going to refuse to go along with the unusual family situation and…

Layla put that fear to rest with her first sentence. "Is there anything I can do from here to help make the transition easier in the morning?"

The three of them talked. About the girls. Deciding on sandals instead of tennis shoes so the girls could get through security. They could put on their own sandals. Determining what Mia would pack in their little backpacks to carry on the plane. Maybe it would be good if Layla had some marshmallows with her, because the twins loved them and they weren't something that would upset their stomachs on the plane.

And then Layla said, "I commend you both. You're making this work. Those are two very lucky little girls."

"*We're* making it work," Mia told the woman she'd once thought of as her mother. "You're a big part in this plan."

"Well then, I have one piece of advice for you."

Mia moved the phone's camera away for a second as she shared a look with Jordon. He didn't seem the least bit concerned. "What's that?" she asked, moving the camera back to get both her and Jordon on-screen.

"Make certain that you don't just support them." Layla's words were clear. But confused Mia.

Jordon was frowning. "You seriously think all I've considered is the money?" Jordon asked the face on the screen.

"No, son, I'm not talking about money at all."

Layla's features were almost ethereal on-screen. The woman exuded peace and wore a happy glow Mia didn't think she'd ever seen before.

"Then what?" Jordon asked.

"Don't be afraid to impose your opinions on them. To make choices that you think are best for them. As they grow up, don't just sit back and support what you think they want. Tell them when you think another choice would be better. Tell them why. And don't ever stop talking to each other about what you think is right for them. More importantly, don't ever stop listening to each other, weighing both sides fairly and equally."

Mia had no idea where any of it was coming from. Or why then. But she welcomed the advice.

And, ironically, the support of her and Jordon's choices.

Jordon, however, was still frowning.

"I don't get it," he said.

"I'm not sure I raised you in the best way I could have, Jordon."

"You're talking nonsense," was his immediate comeback. "What's going on, Ma? What's wrong?"

"Nothing's wrong." Layla's smile was radiant. "But as I watch you two with these little ones, most particularly given your unusual circumstances, I see things I wish I'd done differently. And maybe, had your father lived, I would have."

"You did a great job!" Jordon said then, moving his face closer to the camera to gaze into his mother's eyes. If Mia hadn't been holding the phone, she'd have left the conversation that seemed intimate between a mother and her son.

"Your father thought I coddled you too much, Jordie. He told me to let you explore, to try what wouldn't work so that you could learn what did. It made sense sometimes. Except for the not coddling part. Or maybe I took it too far. After your father died, because you were his son, too, and he could no longer watch out for you, I used his philosophy to raise you. When I wanted to run in and rescue you, or tell you that I didn't agree with something, that I could see pitfalls, I backed off. I watched. I was there to cheer. To pick up pieces…"

The words brought Jordon to tears. Mia could hardly believe the moisture she saw gathering in his eyes as he said, "You were the best, Ma. Don't ever think differently. I was fed. I was loved. I never doubted that I had you at my back every second of every day."

Mia watched. She listened.

And fell in love all over again.

Jordon didn't want to think about his mother. Or taking his daughters from their mother. He wanted to lose himself in the arms of the woman who took his hand and boldly led him down the hall to her room.

Maybe they were playing with flames.

Even if they didn't have sex, the desire between them was going to burn them. Their best shot was to put it out.

And he was willing to work toward that end every night he was with Mia Jones for as long as it took.

Thing was, even after they'd come together twice that night, he felt more on fire for her than he ever had. Maturity brought more to their lovemaking. More confidence, more boldness. More openness to exploration.

They'd used condoms every time they'd been to-gether the past two nights. They had their children. They could have protected sex for the rest of their lives without endangering either one of them.

But he wasn't ready to leave her.

The past few weeks together…they'd only just begun.

"Can I ask you something?" he whispered in case she was asleep.

"Of course." Her sleepy words washed over him, leaving physical evidence in their wake. They didn't have time for a third go-round. Not and have him be rested enough to deal with whatever came his way when he took two precocious four-year-olds away from their mother, onto an airplane, and introduced them to a whole new world.

And a new bedroom.

The question. No right reason for it to be lingering with him. Yet, there it was.

"Why did you break things off with the professor?" The city guy who was still in Shelter Valley.

"Because he wasn't you."

Her words had him rolling on top of her, and the coupling wasn't slow and gentle that time. He barely got the condom on before she was sliding onto him, moving with him for the seconds it took them both to climax.

Twenty minutes later, he was still awake. Lying there next to her.

"What if I come to New York?" Her sleepy words hit him in the darkness. He'd thought she'd drifted off.

"And do what?" he asked, the question that had been taunting him since she'd first pointed out his lack of consideration for her needs and talents ten years ago.

"My crafting. Videos. Wherever it leads me. Be a mother to our daughters."

She didn't mention being a wife to him.

He noticed. Felt another tightening inside him.

"We could just try it out," she suggested. "Maybe I fly home a week or two every month. To see Brilliant. Help Mariah Macy's Mom with the horses. Spend time with families at the dude ranch. See my friends…"

As her list grew, Jordon knew that he couldn't pull his wildflower up from her roots. While the mother in her would thrive for the time the girls were with them, years would pass fast. And parts of what he loved about Mia would wither and die.

He wasn't going to repeat the past. He loved her too much to knowingly fail to put her needs on an equal footing with his.

He told her as much. And finished with, "We'll make it work, Mia." His words were a promise as he pulled her up against him and kissed her softly.

And hoped to God he wasn't lying to her again.

Chapter Twenty-Four

Mia didn't sleep much that night. She knew when Jordon finally drifted off. He'd always made a little noise in his throat during sleep. Not at all a snore, just a small, comforting sound that came from the deepness of his breathing.

She listened.

And she thought a lot, too.

He was right about her not being as personally fulfilled, as personally at home, in New York as he would be. Her career needs wouldn't be fully met.

But when did you look to your own happiness as to that of your children?

Never. You didn't do that. Not if your children were unhappy. They came first.

Ruby and Violet were excited to get on a plane

like when they visited Mickey and see a new city with ice cream on every corner.

If they turned out to not thrive, then Jordon would be the first to suggest another course. Chances were, they'd do great. Other than the few weeks with her at the ranch, the girls had always been in the big city. Could be they'd turn into total daddy's girls.

She'd consider that a great thing.

Jordon Lawrence was a bone-deep good man.

Lying there beside him, even thinking about the way he'd led her on in the past didn't bring up any recrimination toward him.

What Layla had said that night...about not coddling him. Basically, Jordon had been left to make his own decisions since he was eight years old. Had been taught to take action and make life choices relying on his own direction.

It was no wonder he'd done so with what should have been one of the most important decisions of his life: choosing a forever partner.

And then...choosing how their future would succeed.

He'd been wrong to disregard her.

He knew that and had owned his mistakes.

The biggest point engrossing her that night was that he hadn't made them in a knowingly selfish manner. Nor had he made them maliciously.

And just as clear to her—he was who he was. And she couldn't ask him to be anything different than that. He had to do what he thought was right.

Even if it meant hurting her.

He woke up before dawn. Before the alarm they'd set to give them time to shower before waking the girls.

She'd drifted off a time or two but was conscious when he reached for her and gave him everything she had in the silent coupling that followed.

Afterward, he lay there watching her. Holding her gaze. As though he had more to give. Or needed more.

And she knew.

He wanted a different answer to their future. One that didn't include her going to New York. He'd refused that option.

Which only left one more.

He was waiting for her to get to it.

She couldn't.

"If you'd just ask," he said.

Because he couldn't offer. It wasn't the right choice for him.

Mia shook her head. Got out of bed. Slipped into her bathroom, closing the door behind her without looking back.

They'd been so blessed. They had two happy, healthy daughters who needed them and who wanted to be with them. They had each other again.

And they'd make it work.

He might have moved to Shelter Valley to give it a try if she'd only voiced her desire to have him do so.

But she didn't ask him to stay. She couldn't. Because even if he agreed to do so, she couldn't trust him to be able to keep his promise.

* * *

Jordon could hardly bear to watch as Mia hugged their daughters goodbye. For their sakes, he was upbeat as he climbed into the car to drive them away.

Rolled down the windows, a big grin on his face as he told them to wave goodbye to her.

She'd been grinning, too. He'd caught a glimpse of her trembling lips and told the girls to keep waving until they'd turned off the ranch and Mia was no longer in sight.

Their chatter kept him going all the way to Phoenix, and then there was the distraction of getting through the details of boarding a plane. His mother, sitting right across the aisle from them in first class, helped him entertain the twins on the more than four-hour nonstop flight.

Layla would be staying at the apartment with them for the first bit. And then they'd work out a commuting schedule for her to take up nanny duties.

That first week seemed to run almost too smoothly.

The girls kept asking if it was summer yet. They'd wake in the morning and want to know if they were getting on a plane that day.

They insisted on talking to Mama Mia every night before they'd go to bed. He even heard them tell her they loved her.

Something he'd yet to hear from Ruby and Violet.

They'd loved the preschool he took them to on a trial basis their third day in town, so he enrolled them.

They knew where the ice-cream shop was and

conned him into trips there whenever they could. Layla was with them when they weren't in school and he was at work.

Everything was falling into place just as they'd all planned.

Other than the ache in his gut that just wouldn't dissipate. No matter how many antacids he took.

For the first few nights, he'd refused after-work invitations, but at Layla's urging, he slowly started to get back into the swing of his work life.

More people than he'd expected told him how glad they were to have him home. His office arranged a lunch party to congratulate him on his new daughters, and everyone wanted to know when they'd get to meet Ruby and Violet.

Since he owned the investment firm, people *would* clamor.

The thought, unlike him, gave him pause.

But he made deals like there was no tomorrow, earning not only for his investors, but for his daughters' college funds. He was motivated like never before and after the final bell rang at the end of that week, he was on the phone making plans to open a second firm. He'd been thinking about doing so, and when the right person contacted him, he called back.

He phoned Mia, too. She always answered. But was too busy to talk for long. Her lengthy conversations were with Ruby and Violet. Sometimes he listened in. Others, he left them to themselves. He texted her every morning to let her know how the girls slept.

He had also gotten into the habit of letting her know what they were eating. Not just content, but quantity. She'd paid close attention to their diets in Shelter Valley, and so he did the same.

And then came the morning when neither twin asked if they were getting on a plane. Instead, they argued over whether to wear the purple shorts outfit or the pink one. In an effort to allow them to make as many of their own choices as they could, he'd started their first day in New York by allowing them to choose their clothes.

The day it backfired he made the choice for them. Firmly. They were wearing yellow.

When he turned around to find them both staring at him, with open mouths that were topped by pools of tears in both brown and blue eyes, he stopped.

"What's wrong?" he asked, instantly concerned. They could wear purple shorts with pink tops if that's what they wanted. Or one wear purple and one wear pink.

"You yelled," Violet said, just as Ruby blurted, "I want Mama Mia."

That's when Jordon's world spun.

And toppled.

Mia's entire life had been spent in Shelter Valley. But she didn't revolve around that world. She lived for the people in her heart. That included the many friends that were like family to her in the small town that had embraced her since birth. It included the women who came forward to help when her mother died, to step in and be a mother to her on occasion. But in terms of her greatest happiness, she had to be with the people who needed her most. And that summer's end, two of the people closest to her heart weren't yet old enough to choose where they lived. The third was old enough but couldn't choose for her.

She didn't ask a second time if she could move to New York.

Didn't even tell him she was on her way.

She just made arrangements with all of the people she'd served throughout her life to help her keep the ranch thriving while she spent the next several years living on the East Coast for several months during the year.

She'd fly home at least once a month.

And she'd be at the ranch full-time from May through August.

She cried as she hugged Brilliant goodbye. Couldn't bring herself to face Mariah Montford for a final moment. They'd made their promises to each other the day Mariah had overheard her talking to Brilliant. The day that Ruby had called to tell her that Jordon had yelled at them.

She didn't doubt for a second that Jordon had been right to discipline the girls. Didn't fault him for a raised voice.

But she understood that the man was struggling. He needed help.

And was not going to ask for it.

Jordon made his choices and forged ahead with them, making the most of what he had. It was all he knew.

She cried all the way to Phoenix. On and off. And in the airport waiting for her flight. But she didn't question her decision. Or the rightness of it.

For the first time since she'd first seen Ruby and Violet, since she'd seen Jordon again, her heart felt whole. Healthy.

She knew who she was. And who she wanted to be.

Afraid that Layla would tell Jordon she was coming, Mia didn't warn anyone of her imminent arrival. If they weren't overjoyed to see her, she could always turn around and go home.

Already homesick for the ranch, she was looking at that option as a viable one. Going back to the original plan she and Jordon had agreed upon.

But only if the first choice didn't work.

They'd decided to settle for second best.

Giving up on the first option in case it didn't work. Letting it fail before they'd even given it a chance.

They had to at least try.

That was who she and Jordon were. They gave their all to what they most wanted and needed. They weren't people who settled without trying.

Neither of them would ever want their daughters

to view them as people who gave up before giving the best choice a chance.

Armed to the hilt with her mental artillery, she took a cab to Jordon's office the Friday afternoon of his second full week in the city, and stood there, her small roller bag beside her, waiting for him to exit.

The bell had rung. He could be any minute. It might be an hour. She knew he was there. She'd called to find out.

Without introducing herself.

As soon as she knew for sure that she was staying—she couldn't, after all, force him to keep her—she was to text Mariah Montford, who was going to ship the rest of the stuff Mia had packed.

And she didn't want the girls involved in his choice. That wasn't fair to any of them.

She'd thought it all through. Considered every eventuality.

Except one.

Jordon came out of his office carrying a big moving box.

He didn't even see her as he stepped to the curb to hail a cab.

"Jordon?"

He seemed to freeze. Just stood there, facing the curb, holding his box.

Rolling her bag over, she stood beside him. Looked at his box.

He stared at her, white and seemingly shell-shocked.

"Mia?"

They'd texted that morning. About the girls' good night's sleep and breakfast.

She could understand his surprise.

But the box?

"I've moved to New York," she told him, while cabs stopped, others got in them and then pulled away. People milled. Someone even called out to Jordon.

"Good luck!" she heard. Saw him wave.

"You what?" he asked, as he balanced his box between one arm and his torso and used the other hand to pull her back from the curb and up to the high-rise that housed his office. He shook his head. "I can't believe you're here," he said, opening the door and ushering her inside.

Hurrying to keep up with him, Mia said, "We don't settle, Jordon. We have to try for the first choice before we settle for second," she added, afraid she was making no sense at all.

Was he angry she'd come?

That hadn't even been a possibility on her radar.

As she realized that there were many possibilities of which she hadn't thought, Mia tried to rein in her emotions. To think.

She should have called.

Given him a choice, not just shown up on his doorstep.

Thank God she hadn't waited for him outside his apartment building, possibly letting the girls get a glimpse of her.

By the time she had her wits about her, he'd had them in an elevator packed with other people, and then, on the sixteenth floor, typed in a code to let them into a suite of offices. People stopped and stared, she was pretty sure, as Jordon strode toward the only door to the left of the suite's outer door. He held the door for her, motioning her inside before him.

To a room with a large desk, some nice leather furniture, a wet bar…but nothing that spoke of occupancy.

The desktop was completely empty.

He'd shown her to a guest office?

Dropping his box on the massive desktop, Jordon reached for her, pulling her toward him. Her bag came with her at first, until she let go to hold on to the love of her life.

He kissed her, long and not at all gently. He kissed her with hunger.

With a passion he'd never shown her before.

For a long moment, she lost herself in it. Until she pulled her mouth away.

She had no idea what was going on with him. Where he'd been off to with that box, but at least she knew he wanted her still.

That he was glad to see her.

Parts of him were very glad, she noted, as he pressed his expensively clad hips up against her travel-weary jeans.

And kissed her again. Taking her with him to the world where no one existed but them.

When he finally pulled his lips from hers, she saw the tears in his eyes again. Not enough to fall. But the emotion he held there…it was a sight she was going to cherish forever.

"I'm moving to Arizona," he told her then, leaning down to her slightly as he held her shoulders and looked her in the eye. "I love you so much for doing this, Mia. God, you have no idea how much…but you don't belong in the city…"

No. He was not going to send her… "Did you just say you're moving to Arizona?"

"Yeah." He grinned then, looking like the Jordon who'd asked her out on their very first date so many years before. "When I was in Phoenix, I met with a group of investors who told me that if I'd ever want to open an office in Phoenix, they'd see that I had enough business to make it worthwhile. I'd done some trades for one of them."

"You're moving to Phoenix?" Oh, thank God. She could be an hour's drive from home and…

"I'm opening an office in Phoenix," he told her. "I was hoping to be moving to Shelter Valley. I kind of already told Ruby and Violet that they were getting on a plane in the morning to see Mama Mia, but to keep it secret."

"And Macy," she said, without a thought in her head. "They'll see Macy."

Her girls were coming home? She couldn't quite

grasp the joy. It hung there. Teasing her with possibility, but she couldn't accept it for herself.

"What about Layla?"

"She's already put her condominium on the market and has Gloria working with a Realtor in Phoenix, checking out houses."

She couldn't believe it.

Didn't want to let herself try.

But she wasn't a quitter. Or one who settled.

"I'll live in Phoenix, Jordon," she said. Rambling on about her heart and serving those closest to her heart. About the plans she'd made for the ranch to survive without her during the years' worth of several months she had to be gone each time.

Through it all, he just kept shaking his head. But he seemed to be listening to every single word.

And then, when she finally quieted, he said, "I grew up with very little stability, Mia. And no security, other than the surety of my mother's love. You, on the other hand, grew up with more wealth than I could ever have imagined. I just couldn't see it ten years ago. I want our daughters to have such a deep sense of belonging they can survive whatever heartache life brings. Whether it be the loss of their parents. Or the betrayal of the love of your life."

He wasn't speaking about the girls, then.

And as her eyes filled with tears, Mia finally understood how someone could be so exquisitely, beautifully, peacefully happy that they overflowed with it.

"But you love New York…" She couldn't let go of his right to live his best life.

"I needed New York. And I enjoy big-city life, which we'll get plenty of, I can promise you. I'm keeping the apartment here, for now. And I'll be commuting every day to the office in Phoenix. But what I *love*, who I love, is you. And the daughters you insisted we create." He shook his head. "Thank God for you, Mia. For the confidence you've always had to stand up for what your heart tells you is right. You believed so wholeheartedly that we'd have our own children that you wanted to share the glorious opportunity with someone who couldn't provide their own children for themselves. And in so doing, you gave us back the chance to have our own children."

"I just loved you so much and wanted to be sure that I never forgot to be grateful," she told him. "And to share my blessings."

There was so much more to say.

And, apparently, more flying to do in very short order.

Most importantly, there were two little girls who'd need dinner and a bedtime story soon.

Girls who, according to Jordon, just wanted to go home. "Ever since I yelled at them, all they can talk about is going home," he told her. "Home to Mama Mia. And Macy. And our cabin. We'll have to work on that last part," he finished with a grin.

"They didn't seem to mind being in the house that last night, when they knew you were home."

The last night he'd slept with her.

"I can't wait to get there again, Mia. Like them, all I can think, every day, is getting home to Shelter Valley. To the ranch. To you. I love what I do, but coming back with the girls, and not you, I just felt... empty. Speaking of which, the girls and I are on a flight out at six in the morning."

A flight that, luckily, had an open seat left in first class for Mia. Which Jordon booked.

"So... I'm assuming this means...our engagement is back on?" she asked him when he'd finalized the flight transaction on his phone.

What Jordon did next perplexed her all over again. He went rummaging in the box on the desk. And eventually came up with a faded purple ring box.

She was afraid to believe...couldn't believe...but it looked like...

"I've kept this with me since the day you gave it back," he said, opening it. "Locked in the safe here, ever since I opened my own business. Not that it needed a safe," he added, with a sheepish grin as he opened the box. "I'll get you a new one as soon as we..."

Crying again, shaking her head, Mia took the box. "No, Jordon," she said, pulling the tiny, single solitaire diamond set in sterling silver out of the box. "This is the one I want. It's all I ever wanted."

He took it from her. Slid it onto her finger.

They only had hours to get to his apartment, get

the things settled there, get some rest and head to the airport.

But Mia still took the time to slide her arms around Jordon, lay her head on his chest and finally believe, with all her heart, that they'd found their home.

Not in Shelter Valley or New York.

But in each other.

* * * * *

#2995 A MAVERICK REBORN
Montana Mavericks: Lassoing Love • by Melissa Senate

Handsome loner cowboy Bobby Stone has his issues—from faking his own death three years ago to discovering a twin brother he never knew. But headstrong rodeo queen Tori Hawkins is just the woman to break through his tough facade. First with a rambunctious fling...and later with the healing love Bobby's always needed...

#2996 RANCHER TO THE RESCUE
Men of the West • by Stella Bagwell

Mack Barlow may have broken Dr. Grace Hollister's heart in high school, but sparks still fly when the now-single father walks into her medical clinic. His young daughter is adorable. And he's...too dang sexy by far! Can a very busy divorced mom take a second chance on loving the man who once left her behind?

#2997 OLD DOGS, NEW TRUTHS
Sierra's Web • by Tara Taylor Quinn

When heiress Lindsay Warren-Smythe assumes a false identity to meet her biological father, she's not expecting to develop a connection with her new coworker, Cole Bennet, and his lovable dog. Cole has learned the hard way not to trust beautiful liars with his heart, so when he lets his guard down with Lindsay, will her lies tear them apart?

#2998 MATCHMAKER ON THE RANCH
Forever, Texas • by Marie Ferrarella

Rancher Chris Parnell has known Rosemary Robinson all his life. But working side by side with the beautiful vet to diagnose the sickness affecting his cattle kicks him completely out of his friend zone! Roe can't deny the attraction sizzling between them. But will her friend with benefits stick around once the cattle mystery is solved?

#2999 HER YOUNGER MAN
Sutton's Place • by Shannon Stacey

Widow Laura Thompson falling for a younger man? Not on your life! Except Riley Thompson is so dang charming. And handsome. And everything Laura's missing in her life. The town seems to be against their romance. Including Riley's boss...who's Laura's son! Are Riley and Laura strong enough to take a stand for love?

#3000 IN TOO DEEP
Love at Hideaway Wharf • by Laurel Greer

Chef Kellan Murphy is determined to fulfill his sister's dying wish. But placing an ocean-fearing man in a scuba diving class is ridiculous! Instructor Sam Walker can't resist helping the handsome wannabe diver overcome his fears. And their unexpected connection is the perfect remedy for Sam's own hidden pain...

YOU CAN FIND MORE INFORMATION ON UPCOMING HARLEQUIN TITLES, FREE EXCERPTS AND MORE AT HARLEQUIN.COM.

HSECNM0623

Get 3 FREE REWARDS!

We'll send you 2 FREE Books plus a FREE Mystery Gift.

FREE
Value Over
$20

Both the **Harlequin® Special Edition** and **Harlequin® Heartwarming™** series feature compelling novels filled with stories of love and strength where the bonds of friendship, family and community unite.

HARLEQUIN
PLUS

Try the best multimedia
subscription service for romance
readers like you!

Read, Watch and Play.

Experience the easiest way to get
the romance content you crave.

Start your **FREE TRIAL** at
<u>www.harlequinplus.com/freetrial</u>.